CHILL

Copyright © 1978 by Jory Sherman

An original Pinnacle Books edition, published for the first time anywhere.

First printing, December 1978

ISBN: 0-523-40221-X

Cover illustration by Jack Thurston

Printed in the United States of America

PINNACLE BOOKS, INC.
2029 Century Park East
Los Angeles, California 90067

## The Flow of Death

The funny thing was that Joan didn't look as if she were in any danger. Her breathing, though slow, was regular. So was her pulse. There had been no change on the chart. The same with the blood pressure. She was such a beautiful girl. A sleeping beauty. That's what she reminded her of—Sleeping Beauty, like a fairy tale. Well, it would take more than a handsome prince to wake this one up.

Bernice Baines was walking away from Joan's bed when she noticed the I.V. apparatus.

The bottle of I.V. solution was completely covered with a sticky green mold. So was the stand from which it hung. Mrs. Baines ran around the side of the bed and looked down at the floor. Starting from the window, there was a six-inch-wide stream of what appeared to be green slime leading to the I.V. stand. It seemed to be fed by some force that pushed it up the stand.

Her eyes went to the tube where I.V. solution dripped into Joan's veins. She shook her head as if to clear her eyes. Blindly, she reached for the tubing. Her hand seemed to move in slow motion, although her mind was screaming at her to hurry. She grabbed at the tubing, missing it on the first try. She lashed out again, her hand finally grasping the plastic tubing inches from the needle in Joan's arms. She tugged, and the needle came loose.

Seconds later, a flow of green slime, which was mingled with the intravenous solution, oozed from the tip of the needle. . . .

The "CHILL" Series:

*Satan's Seed*
*Chill*

*Chill*

*Jory Sherman*

**PINNACLE BOOKS**          **LOS AN**

For Bill and Don and the life support system of Dogwood Hills—including the people who make it all work, our friends.

# CHILL

# CHAPTER ONE

There it was again. She looked quickly away from the house.

The tug at her abdomen, the tilt of the ground, the giddiness. The wicker basket at her feet seemed so far away. She drew a breath and stood up in her garden, trying to get a fix on the horizon. She looked down at the neat rows of vegetables, and the straight lines seemed to curve.

It was the house.

Every time she looked at it too long, this dizziness assailed her senses, this awful wave of sickness came over her. It wasn't sickness, exactly. It was more like a sickening premonition of fear, of dread.

The nausea would pass. It always did—after she looked away from the house.

She tried to align the horizon, to stabilize her senses. Her forehead was drenched with sweat. Not perspiration—sweat. Streams of it trickled into her eyes. She wiped the moisture away. Her brows were soaked. The horizon danced for a long moment, then steadied.

For a week it had been like this: the ground turning to rubber underneath her feet, the house seeming to move—imperceptibly—every time she looked at it. Maybe there was too much white against the green

1

landscape. It was a big, old house—a mansion, really. But she and Tom loved it. Six months ago, they had inherited it. Well, she had. They thought it perfect, a summer place, their own acknowledgment of the back-to-the-land movement. It was their retreat from the hectic, scrambling world of television production.

It was a week ago that she had first pitched forward into the garden, feeling off-balance and disoriented. She nearly fainted. And she had rushed into town, 15 miles away, to see the doctor: Stanley Morgan, M.D.

"It's probably not Ménière's disease, although the symptoms are similar," he had said. Kindly Dr. Morgan, one of Shreveport's finest. A friend of a friend. Middle-aged and paunchy, with those huge horn-rimmed glasses, a bristly moustache, and fat, sensuous, multicolored lips that were too small for his face and too wet to look at.

"What's Ménière's disease?" Patty Brunswick had asked. "I've never heard of it."

"It's what you likely don't have, Patty," Dr. Morgan had said, laughing. "A pressure in the balancing mechanism of the ear. You probably don't have it. It usually comes with age—between forty and sixty, and men get it more often than women. You can hear out of both ears all right, can't you?"

She could.

"The disease usually brings on deafness. No deafness here. No tinnitus?"

"Tinnitus?"

"Ringing in the ears. Buzzing. Hissing. No strange noises in your head?"

"No, none of that. Only the giddiness and the dizzy spells."

"Your symptoms are probably psychological. I

2

mean, I could send you to an ear, eyes, nose, and throat man, but I think it would be a waste of time and money. Any unusual excitement lately? Any emotional upheavals out there at your place?"

Dr. Morgan knew that she had inherited the Grandier place from a great-uncle she'd never really known. And he knew that she and her husband were really out of their element. The place was so run down. Bernard Grandier had been a recluse, and no one had seen him for the last several years of his life.

"No, Stan," she had said. "Nothing big. Oh, it's Joan's birthday this coming Sunday. We're having a few friends out over the weekend. I'm planning a big party on Saturday."

"Hmmm, I thought maybe the country life had gotten to both of you. Chiggers, ticks, mosquitoes, cottonmouths. Can be a shock to city folk."

Patty had laughed.

"Well, I don't like the bugs, but you get used to them. And, no, Stan, Tom and I aren't fighting, if that's what you're thinking. Tom thinks the house is just great. He's been reading *Mother Earth News* ever since Chill gave him a copy."

"He's that psychic fellow your husband did a television program on, isn't he?"

"Yes. Chill and Tom are good friends. Anyway, Chill isn't really psychic. He just investigates supernatural stuff."

"Then you two really are happy out there?"

"Sure, so why am I dizzy?"

"Maybe you're going through the 'change' a little early," Morgan had said. "What are you, thirty-nine? . . ."

"Ah, call it thirty-nine, Stan. I'm forty-one. And I'm

not getting hot flashes. I'm still attracted to Tom. And I had a hysterectomy five years ago."

"I see. Okay, Patty, I'll give you some pills. Call me in a week if you have any more spells. You may be allergic to the sun. You only get this when you're outdoors?"

Had she told him that? Probably. It was true.

The nurse had given her a packet of pills with instructions scrawled on the white envelope: *Take one if dizziness occurs.*

She fumbled for the pills in her pocket. Did she have them with her? They were big as horse pills, and she wondered if she could swallow one without any water. Besides, she was feeling better now. It wasn't exactly dizziness, anyway—well, sort of. She had told Dr. Morgan she felt dizzy. That had been the only way she could describe it then.

Now, however, she knew it was more. Her stomach had turned over. She had the distinct impression the house had moved.

But that was impossible, wasn't it?

Patty looked up at the serene blue sky. Should she take the pill?

Tom didn't know about her visit to Dr. Morgan. She didn't want to worry him. Tom would turn it into a major clinical investigation. He had worried himself sick over her hysterectomy. Well, they had thought she might have cancer, but she hadn't—only an infection of the uterus. So it had been removed. No more children. But Joan was child enough. She had filled both their lives. She would be sixteen on Sunday. The party was to be a surprise for her. Some young friends, some neighbor children, Tom's friends from New Orleans, Chill, a single female for him (Tom's idea), and it would all be very gay and pleasant.

4

So why was she having these feelings of queasiness?

Anxiety. Maybe she was emotionally overwrought—too excited about the party, too anxious to show off the place, to show the guests what they had done in just six happy, busy months. The garden, especially, was her pride and joy, and Tom's too. The vegetables served at the party would be only those they had grown themselves. They had only about a quarter acre under cultivation, but the rich soil was producing more vegetables than the three of them could eat. She was canning, too, and that was a new and rewarding experience. She had put up beans already, and soon she would be able to can squash, tomatoes, corn, and a host of other home-grown vegetables she could serve next winter with pride.

*Did she dare look at the house again?*

What was so frightening about it? It was an old house, but not ugly. In fact, despite its disrepair, it was quite beautiful. It was like any number of old Southern plantation mansions—two stories, gables, stately columns on the front porch—but she never could get the style of architecture straight. Greek, she supposed, or maybe it was Roman—perhaps a combination of both. The front lawn was huge, wide and long, bordered and inset with flower beds.

Old Moses Petitjean had taken care of the grounds for years, and he was still there—he came with the Grandier place.

The interior of the house was shabby, but that contributed to its decadent charm. The house was of another time, another world. It was deliciously anachronistic, and Tom had fallen in love with it from the first. It was similar, in fact, to Chill's place up near Atlanta, although his was reputed to be elegant. She had never been to his home, but Tom had featured a shot of it in his documentary about Chill. The documentary was still playing in new markets and rerunning in the original ones, Tom had told her.

Why was she thinking of Chill just now? Because he was arriving tomorrow? Or because she thought there was something strange, something off-key about the house? Well, she liked Chill. He was handsome and charming—sexy, even. But just because she liked him didn't mean she could believe the world was inhabited by ghosts and demons. There was something worldly about Chill, yet unworldly at the same time. She couldn't see herself talking to him about her problem, but maybe she would. It might be interesting to hear his theory.

She let her eyes drift over the landscape. She loved the stately trees, the big oaks and hickory trees. There was a pecan grove and another orchard where peaches and plums hung on leafy branches. There were apple trees as well. To her right, the land was densely wooded and overgrown, rising to a green bluff that overlooked that section of the property. She had inherited more than 200 acres, and they had seen but a small portion of it. She and Tom had both vowed to pack a picnic lunch one day and take Joan and explore the property. But so far, they hadn't taken the time. Besides, the density of the undergrowth was somewhat forbidding, even formidable.

She must get back to picking the vegetables for their evening salad.

It was silly to think that the house had made her feel so odd. Well, she just wouldn't look at it again until she was through. She took a deep breath and bent over to pick some more radishes. They were thick and needed thinning; some were starting to

6

split. She picked a dozen, then walked over to the lettuce bed. Bibb lettuce was the only variety she could get to grow. Head lettuce grew straight up but wouldn't come to a head. She tore a few leaves off and put them in her wicker basket. She picked some fragrant coriander. Tom had planted that. He loved coriander. He'd called it *cilantro*, however, ever since he'd done that documentary in Mexico. Tom told her the Mexicans used it in their cooking. "Chinese parsley," some people called it. It was aromatic. She held a leaf to her nose and sniffed deeply. The scent of it seemed to clear her head. It was difficult, if not impossible, to buy, so they grew their own.

She felt better. She plucked a ripe bell pepper from its mooring. Its deep green color was almost hypnotic. She would cut up part of it for the salad. The rest could go into the pot roast for Sunday.

Patty lifted the basket. She had picked enough. Why was she hesitating, then? She would have to go back to the house sometime. She looked off toward the end of the garden. Beyond was the huge barn, almost empty now. They had no cattle, no livestock—just the cats that Abigail Dailey, their cook, kept around the house to keep the rat and mouse population under control.

She looked once again out over the bottomland. Tom said they should try to cultivate more of it next year. It was a shame to let such good land go to waste. Honestly, she wondered if he was reverting to a country boy—which he never had been until she had inherited this huge place from her father's uncle. She was the only heir, apparently, and that was that. Still, it had been a shock. There were no liens or mortgages on the property. The taxes were low. There had been some money, too, which had been enough to pay off the inheritance tax.

She remembered her great-uncle Bernard Grandier, but hadn't seen him since she was a child. Her parents, Norman and Ida Grandier, had spoken of him little during their last years.

The attorney had been tight-lipped, the officious type. A small man with a thin moustache and a bristly, cockroachy manner, scurrying amid piles of ancient, dusty papers in an old, smelly office. He had handled the Grandier affairs for years. "Here's the deed, Mrs. Brunswick, and the check from the trust account. It's all in order. Thank you." Good-bye. Like that.

His name was Pierre Duchamps. When she had called his office, the intercept operator told her that the phone had been disconnected and was no longer in service. The office in Shreveport was now occupied by a mail-order firm. Mr. Duchamps, it appeared, had retired. Address unknown. The letter she had mailed had been returned: "Undeliverable as addressed."

She had never seen a copy of the will.

Patty turned, lowering her eyes. She picked her way through the rows, heading on an oblique angle back toward the house. The soil between the rows was nicely manicured, thanks to Tom and his motor-driven tiller. The weeds grew insanely after every rain, and if he didn't keep after them, they would take over the garden—like those vines that grew near the bluff and crawled up the oak trees, which shaded the house. Nature was possessive in Louisiana. Without the tilling, the vegetation would choke out the garden.

She would have to look up at the house. She couldn't avoid it. She stepped over the last row and walked along the fence to the garden gate. They had put up wire mesh to keep the rabbits out, then planted peas and beans along the fence so the plants could climb the wire. The peas had been planted too late and had not done well. The beans, though, had grown over the fence and become entwined in their own tendrils. She opened the gate.

The basket was heavy in her hand. The house was not far now. She took another deep breath, letting it out quickly as her stomach knotted up. She should have worn a sunbonnet. It would have shaded her head and face, kept her from . . . from what? Looking at the house again?

She wanted to laugh at herself. Tom would, she knew. He would think she had stayed out in the sun too long. Maybe that was it . . . maybe it was the sun's heat that made her lightheaded, dizzy. She took a step and looked up at the house. For a moment it seemed small and far away. She squinted into the sun. The house stood out in relief. It was like looking through an old-fashioned stereopticon.

Maybe it was that expanse of white that made her react so strangely. The white walls of the house glared in the sunlight, against the green of the foliage, of the trees, surrounding it. She stared, transfixed, wondering if she had conquered her hysteria.

She took a step toward the house, her shoulders rising with a deep breath. She would not let the hysteria grip her this time. *Forewarned was forearmed. Mind over matter.* The clichés piled up, comforting little adages that gave her a grip on reality despite their triteness. She needed them. She needed *something!*

The earth tipped underneath her feet, like an unsteady table.

The house turned into a rubbery image, and she

saw the sky shimmer before it began to spin wildly above the roof. Blue and white and green kaleidoscoped, and she felt herself falling backward, the basket of vegetables flung spastically from her hand. She screamed in terror.

She hit the ground with a thud, her scream blown into silence by the sudden impact. Her eyes brimmed over with stinging tears.

"Tommmmmm!" she shrieked, when her wind returned. "Tommmmmmmmmmmmm!"

She saw the stone wall that bordered the backyard patio, the umbrellas, the lawn underneath her stretching out like some turbulent swollen sea. The house blurred and expanded, seemed to grow larger, seemed to rush up toward her as nausea curdled up from her stomach.

Through it all, she thought she saw the back door open and Tom running toward her. From the corner of her eye, she saw, or thought she saw, another figure in slow motion. A strange dark man in overalls and a straw hat, carrying a stick, a hoe, a scythe—something big. Moses Petitjean. Yes. And Tom, far away—he was coming, too. She fought to hold on, to keep from vomiting.

# CHAPTER TWO

Everything was terribly mixed up. The images fluttered like moths dancing around a naked light bulb at night. The man running toward her—Tom, she guessed, she hoped—was fragmented, out of focus, out of synchronization with her brain and her eyes.

The voice came to her from far away, a voice pushed through a tin horn. The words fluttered around her, a mass of fragile insects beating their wings on the screen of her consciousness. Some of the syllables came through, then turned into watery bubbles that broke almost before she could grasp them.

"Patty! What happened? Are you all right?"

She recognized Tom's voice. She knew she could shut her eyes now. He would reach her any moment, any hour. It didn't make any difference. The house was fading. She locked her eyelids shut and waited until the house swam away through the tiny hole at the end of the tunnel of darkness.

"Moses! Help me get her up. She's not hurt, is she? Patty! Say something, for God's sake!"

She felt herself being lifted up. She could not open her eyes. She wondered if her lips were moving. She was trying to move them, trying to make a sound.

"Tom?"

11

"Oh, Patty, how did you fall? What happened? She's white as a sheet, Moses. Can you walk, honey? Come on, let's carry her to the house. She must have tripped."

She could understand the words now. Moses was there. She felt arms around her. There was no feeling in her legs, but the dizziness was going away. Her feet touched the ground. She tried to put weight on her feet. She couldn't summon the courage to open her eyes.

"Joan!" she heard her husband cry. "Call Dr. Morgan. Quick! Something's happened to your mother. Hurry!"

"Tom, I'm all right. Just get me inside."

"Patty! Can you walk? Did you hurt yourself badly? Joan's calling the doctor. Don't worry, honey, everything's going to be all right."

She felt herself being lifted up the steps to the patio. She felt the flagstones underneath her feet.

"Get the door open, Moses. I can carry her the rest of the way."

At that moment, she loved Tom very much. He was in charge. She trusted him. Tom was so good to her. Her feet felt the wooden threshold rise underneath them. The coolness of the house rushed in on her. The screen door slammed, then the back door.

Patty opened her eyes.

"Tom—help me to the living room. Just let me sit down. I'll be fine in a minute."

She looked into his gray-blue eyes. A shock of red hair framed his lean, handsome face. She reached up with her small hand and threaded her fingers through the thick locks until her fingertips touched his scalp. Tom's body relaxed as he gave a huge sigh of relief.

12

In the living room, Joan was just hanging up the telephone.

"He's coming right out," she said. "Mom, are you okay? Dad, what happened?"

"She's going to be fine, I think." He led her to the couch. The furniture was covered with gleaming brown simulated textured leather. "What happened, Patty?" His voice was tender with concern.

Moses stood in the doorway, a tall, slender black man with gray kinky hair cut short, thin and tufted in cottony patches. He held his straw hat in his hands. His brown eyes were rheumy next to a wide, flat nose with flaring nostrils. White false teeth gleamed from pink plastic gums. His jaw bulged slightly from a lump created by half a thimbleful of Red Seal snuff. His overalls were clean and pressed over a long-sleeved blue chambray shirt that was wearing thin.

"Does you need me, Mistah Brunswick?"

"No, Moses, thanks," said Tom.

"Thank you, Moses," said Patty, managing a weak smile.

"I'll fetch the basket and vegetables," said the black man before striding away.

Patty laughed with relief.

"The vegetables. I forgot all about them. Oh, Tom, what's the matter with me? I feel fine now, but out there . . . I just came unglued."

He looked at her intently. Patty was petite. Some people thought she was frail, but he knew better. She was tiny but strong, in body and in will. Her short, strawlike hair might have seemed tomboyish to some, but she was feminine to a fault. In the dim light she looked scarcely older than their daughter. But Joan was tall and wide-shouldered, with long hair, dark

13

eyes and a square jaw—like him. Patty's eyes were hazel brown, the color of dark mustard, her lips full and sensuous. Tom thought she looked frail at the moment, and that worried him.

"What happened, Patty?" His tone was serious.

She told him. Joan floated to a chair and sat quietly, listening, fascinated with her mother's account of her nausea and dizziness every time she looked at the house. Patty told them of her secret visit to the doctor and of his diagnosis.

"I didn't think we had any secrets from each other," Tom said quietly.

"You would have worried unnecessarily."

"I'm more worried now."

"Why? I feel all right. It's only when I'm outside."

"I know."

"You know?"

"Yes," he said. "The same thing's happened to me, once or twice in the past week."

Patty and Joan exchanged looks.

"Then what's all this about not having secrets from each other?" Patty asked accusingly.

"I'm sorry. I didn't want to worry you, either."

"Oh, you two!" Joan said, grinning. "You're like a couple of love birds."

"Have you had symptoms, Joan?" asked her father.

Joan got up from her seat. "Of course not. I think you're both a couple of hypochondriacs!"

"Have you looked at the house from the outside?" Patty looked at her daughter in disbelief.

"Oh, sure," said Joan, starting across the room. She was wearing white shorts and a halter top and was barefooted. "It's just a tremor. You know, like a small earthquake."

"What?" Tom said. "You've felt it?"

14

"A while ago, I did. A couple of times this week. Maybe the house is settling. It is old, you know."

Patty breathed a sigh of relief.

"Well, at least we're not crazy," she said.

Moses walked in, his hat in his hand.

"I set the basket in the kitchen," he said. "Ain't no settlin' of this old house. This foundation's solid."

"Have you, ah, felt anything strange lately, Moses?" Tom asked.

"I got to get to my flowers," he said gruffly, avoiding Tom.

"Wait a minute," Tom said, striding after Moses. "I want an answer to my question."

Moses turned and gave Tom a look of pained sorrow.

"Ain't no call for you to talk to me thataways, Mistah Brunswick. I does my work and Mistah Grandier, he done ast me to stay on, but I don't has to."

"I—I'm sorry, Moses. Forgive me. It's just that something's going on around here, and we're worried. You've lived here longer than we have."

Moses looked at Tom as though he were a small child or an imbecile.

"Yessah, they's somethin' goin' on 'round here, all right."

There was a palpable tension in the room. Every eye was fixed on Moses, who seemed to be trembling, not visibly, but trembling nevertheless. There was a latent belligerence about him that no one seemed to have noticed before.

"What do you mean by that?" Tom asked.

Moses' lower lip began to quiver.

He said nothing, only glared at Joan.

Patty brought a hand up to her throat. She looked

15

at her daughter, at Moses. *Why was he staring at Joan like that?*

"I think you'd better answer me," Tom said, not at all sure of himself. "What's going on around here? My wife's obviously upset and you keep looking at Joan that way."

Moses raised his arm. It was shaking. He extended a black and pink bony finger. Straight at Joan. Accusing.

"Ask her!" Moses exclaimed. "You wanna know what's goin' on, ask her!"

Joan's body went rigid. Her face blanched white. She stared at Moses, at his accusing finger.

"Joan?" Patty rose to go to her daughter, a queasy churning in her stomach.

Joan opened her mouth, started to say something, then crumpled to the floor in a dead faint.

Patty screamed as the house began to quiver. Tom ran to his daughter and picked her up in his arms. Patty recovered and knelt beside her husband. They looked up at Moses, but he was gone.

They both heard the distant rumbling. The house shook as if a mighty force was coursing through its concrete, its wood and plaster.

The sound of its shuddering was something like laughter. Insane laughter.

# CHAPTER THREE

The two-toned station wagon drifted into the gravel-packed circular drive, its white-walled tires crunching the stones as it pulled past the sidewalk and came to a stop behind two parked cars, a red Corvette and a dark green Ford LTD. The door opened, and a tall man stepped out into the morning sunshine. He wore aviator-type sunglasses to keep the glare from his eyes. He was trim and muscled in a short-sleeved light blue tennis shirt and dark blue double-knit slacks. His shoes were white textured-leather Florsheim loafers.

He reached a deeply tanned arm into the back seat and pulled forth a small Vuitton bag. This carried his papers, notebooks, and personal items. From the floor he lifted another small case, this one containing two pistols. Both pistols were loaded. He carried them with him, along with any other firearms he might be using, almost everywhere he went.

Chill shut the door, walked back down the gravel drive, and took in the surroundings. On one side of the house, there was a swimming pool sunk into the manicured lawn. Wooden tables with umbrellas, and webbed chairs and lounges were scattered around the pool. The water, shimmering invitingly, was lime-green in the sun. There was a large garage on the other side of the house. Tom's Mercedes 300 SL was in one of the spaces, Patty's Pontiac station wagon in the other. A new Chevrolet pickup was parked outside.

Chill turned up the walkway and looked at the stately columns that supported the roof, the upper dormers breaking up the expanse of shingles. The house reminded him of his own, only this one was smaller.

He was halfway up the walkway, when the front door opened.

"Chill!" Tom Brunswick walked out on the porch, thin, nervous, his red hair flared out like an explosion in a wig factory.

Chill raised a hand in greeting. He sensed, however, that something was wrong. It was too quiet, and he could have sworn that Tom's greeting had been just loud enough to carry, little more than an amplified whisper. Tom still affected the Hollywood hyphenate's garb, even out in the country, the writer-director-producer's Gucci loafers, the chino pants, the garish sport shirt. But Chill saw the worry lines on Tom's forehead, the forced smile, the dullness in the blue-gray eyes, the dark circles underneath.

"Tom."

"You're early, thank God. I've been trying to reach you. Mrs. Ryerson said you had a phone in your wagon. She gave me the mobile number, but I couldn't reach you. Rather, the operator couldn't."

Chill stepped up onto the porch and took Tom's extended hand. There was no force in the producer's grip. Chill felt as if Tom was unaware of the handshake, just acting automatically. At close range, he could see the tightness around Tom's mouth, the skin

18

drawn taut over his cheeks and jaw. Tom looked distracted, haunted.

"The phone went out. I wasn't aware of it until I tried to call ahead. Sorry. I'll call Maude after a while and tell her I got in all right." Maude Ryerson was Chill's middle-aged girl Friday, a doughty grayhaired woman who acted as secretary and housekeeper at his home.

"Thought you were flying down, Chill."

"I decided to drive, but you don't want to hear all this. What's wrong, Tom?"

"Come on in the house," Tom said tightly. "Jeez, I'm glad to see you, man." He put his arm around Chill's shoulder and squeezed it. He ushered the taller man inside and closed the door. It was very quiet inside the house, and Chill thought that strange. He set down his bag and followed Tom across the hardwood floor of the foyer. He kept the light-brown case holding the pistols with him, even though it was locked. He would keep it with him until he could leave it in his room.

A wide staircase flowed upward to the second floor, which was ringed by a balcony railing. Doorways branched off the foyer. They passed a coat rack, incongruous in the heat of summer, but dignified as old relics made of wood can be when they are so highly polished. The floor reflected their dark figures. Potted plants lined the bare wall. Near the staircase, there was a bureau with a telephone on top of it. In a room to his left, Chill caught a glimpse of mirrors and a portion of a table. He guessed the room was one of the dining rooms, perhaps the main one. The doors upstairs were all closed. Six bedrooms, at least, he figured.

The living room was spacious, fitted with a bar, the

19

vinyl-covered furniture gleaming with a high, nut-colored sheen. There was a baby grand piano in one corner, and the bookshelves, lining the room, were full. One section contained Tom's television scripts, which were bound in Moroccan leather.

A maple drop-leaf teacart was set with a cut-crystal brandy bottle and glasses. Four spindle-backed Beechwood stools stood in front of the slate-topped bar, which had brown vinyl on the front and sides. There were various bottles in a cabinet in back of the bar, and on the top there was a small wooden tub filled with fresh lemons. Other cabinets held more books, statuettes of awards Tom had won for his documentaries: plates, nicknacks, mugs, a globe of the world, and ceramic figurines. Everything seemed neat and tidy.

Chill noticed the glassed-in cabinet where several film cans gleamed on wide shelves. Tom had made himself a home here. It was quite a change from the temporary home the Brunswicks had occupied in the San Fernando Valley. They had never been able to settle down in the Los Angeles area. Things were too hectic out there. The Brunswick driveway was always full of cars, the living room full of writers, members of the crew, actors, actresses, and hangers-on.

"Have a chair, Chill," Tom said. "I have to talk to you for a few minutes before we go upstairs. The doctor's up there now. He was here yesterday and last night. Came back early this morning. I just don't understand it."

"I think you ought to sit down too, Tom."

"Yeah, I guess I'm pretty nervous."

Chill sat in a chair. Tom plunked himself down on the love seat, but couldn't sit back for more than a second and finally settled for the edge of the seat. He wrung his slender hands again and again, as if trying to find a starting point for what he had to say. Finally he looked up at Chill, locked into the man's penetrating gaze. It had never failed to unnerve him, despite the fact that a warm friendship had grown up between them ever since they had worked together on the documentary a few years before.

"I didn't ask you out here to work, Chill," Tom began, "although it's going to look that way. We were going to have a 'Sweet Sixteen' birthday party for Joan."

"So tell me, Tom. Don't hold back." Chill sensed that his friend was about to break up. There was a husky catch in Tom's voice, the prelude to tears.

"I don't know. Everything was just fine. Then Joan fainted yesterday, and the doctor, Stan Morgan, can't find anything wrong with her. Patty's been going through some strange experiences. Me, too, I guess. I'm worried sick. I feel helpless as hell."

Tom broke up, then, and Chill sat there helplessly as his friend sobbed. The sobs came from deep down and tore at Tom's slight frame like jolts of electricity. The sounds were almost unbearable.

Chill waited until the upheaval passed. It subsided as Tom got a grip on his emotions. Chill had seen men cry before. Usually, they kept things bottled up inside so long that when the flood burst, it acted as a purgative as well as a calmative. Tom was strong-willed ordinarily, Chill knew, so whatever had jolted him had to be serious.

"I'm all right now," Tom said. "It's hell to cry like this in front of a friend."

"No it isn't. It's the best place to do it."

"Thanks." The smile was weak, but it was there.

"Feel like talking about it now, Tom?"

21

"I guess so. Yeah . . . I have to get it out, tell someone. It all started a week ago." Tom told Chill of Patty's experiences with the house, and of his own, and how they had both kept it a secret from the other, out of a false concern.

"Then, when Moses looked at Joan and pointed at her—she just fainted. I don't know if he scared her or not. I've been afraid of talking to the man. He's so sensitive. We sort of inherited him with the place."

"I'll talk to him, if you'd like."

"Would you? Oh, that'd be great. Dr. Morgan's with Joan now. She hasn't come out of her faint, if that's what it is, and I'm about to explode with the anxiety. I've taken Dexies to keep me going, and Miltowns to calm me down. I feel like I've got a nest of hornets in my head."

"You say these feelings of dizziness only happen when you're outside, looking at this house?"

"That's right. Joan thought it was some kind of earthquake, or maybe the house settling. That could do it, couldn't it? The doctor's checked both Patty and me out, and there's nothing wrong with us. No blood pressure problems or anything like that. I was 140 over 85 this morning. Patty was 128 over 80."

"Any other manifestations? Noises? Apparitions?"

"No."

"Have you had any odd reactions inside the house?"

"Not until yesterday. I mean, when Moses clammed up and then told us to ask Joan about all this stuff, that kind of disturbed us. . . . No, it *really* disturbed us." Tom's hands were beginning to tremble.

"Better lay off the pills, Tom. You've got chemicals building up in your system. That's not going to help your nerves any."

22

"You're the doctor," Tom said, grinning.

Chill was silent, thinking.

Chill, known to many as Russell Chillders, Ph.D., had taken his doctorate at Stanford. He was not a psychic himself, but he had been interested in the occult for many years. Born under the truth-seeking sign of Aquarius, he was now in his early thirties. His father, Judson Chillders, was a farmer, retired for the most part. Chill's mother, Carrie, was dead, but had been psychically gifted. One summer, when Chill was quite young, he had gone to Europe, where he stayed with his mother's brother, Martin Stamm, in Vienna.

At his uncle Martin's house, Chill participated in strange rites that his uncle called "raising the spirits." The experiences had scared Chill half out of his wits, but he was impressed. He participated in candle rites and read a great many of his uncle's books on the occult. Uncle Martin had died a few years after Chill's mother passed away, but before his death, he had told the young man that he had no fear. He believed that life would go on in another dimension. Chill had spent most of his adult life trying to prove that his uncle Martin had been right.

Uncle Martin had been a strong factor, but Chill had also been influenced by a book he stumbled upon. It was an early but up-to-date account of Dr. T. K. Oesterreich's *Occultism in This Modern Age*, published in 1928. Later, Chill did extensive research at the Edgar Cayce Foundation in New York and at Virginia Beach. He had been very impressed by the Cayce material and by the life of the seer. He later studied under Eileen Garrett, who was at that time president of the Parapsychology Foundation of New York, a worldwide organization that encouraged and supported scientific investigations and studies in the realm of extrasensory perception. Through Ms. Garrett, Chill met a number of nonprofessional mediums, who helped launch him on his career of investigating the supernatural.

His investigations took him deep into the occult world. While he retained his native skepticism, he also came to believe that there had been superordinary, inexplicable events throughout history and continuing into the present. He began to be recognized as an authority on the occult, mainly through his books, two of which he wrote after he met Laura Littlefawn, a half-Sioux psychic.

Chill had made numerous television appearances in connection with his latest books, *The Case for Reincarnation* and *Steps Beyond the Veil*, and consequently was well-known to television audiences. Few people, however, knew that he had served as a Green Beret in the early days of the Vietnam war. He had resigned his commission and refused all subsequent offers of employment by the C.I.A. Working with the Montagnards, however, had whetted his curiosity about primitive weapons, and Chill had a keen interest in black-powder rifles and pistols. He had built many replicas that were authentic recreations of Kentucky and Pennsylvania rifles. He was a top-notch trap shooter, a skilled bowman, and an expert rifle and pistol shot. These things, too, he kept to himself for the most part, although he was a member of the National Muzzleloading Rifle Association and often shot the black-powder rifles in competition.

Finally, Chill stood up and paced the floor. He walked with a dancer's grace, a prizefighter's gait, and one guessed he would be a patient stalker in the woods. He stopped and turned to Tom.

"I'd like to stay on here for a few days. I want to

talk to Patty and take a look at your daughter. I'd like to check out this Moses you mentioned, too—perhaps find out more about the history of this mansion. No charge. Is it a deal?"

# CHAPTER FOUR

"It's a deal, Chill. I'd be grateful. So would Patty, although you know she doesn't believe in this supernatural stuff."

"I'd also like to talk to Dr. Morgan."

"We'll go upstairs now. I told Patty you were here. She'll want to see you. They'll be with Joan in her bedroom."

Tom got up, and the two men walked to the door.

"What are you thinking, Chill? Is it something to do with the supernatural?"

Chill looked at his friend as they both paused at the opening to the room.

"Honestly, Tom, I don't know. Whatever's going on here is strange. It's got you and your family on edge. That's enough to make me concerned. Let's say that there is something definitely *unnatural* going on here."

Tom said nothing, and the two men climbed the stairs. Tom turned to the right at the top of the stairs and led Chill to the last doorway on the right.

"This is Joan's room," he whispered.

The phone began ringing. Tom made no move to answer it. It stopped in the middle of the third ring.

"I have an office upstairs. Kim's here taking the calls. She got in late last night."

"Kim? Here?"

"She's been coming up from New Orleans on week-ends." Kim was Kim Michaels, Tom's administrative assistant for Brunswick Productions. She had been with Tom for about two years. Chill had met her the year before at KTTV in Los Angeles, while Tom was producing a television show there. Chill remembered Kim. She was an attractive blonde, tall, graceful, and intelligent.

Tom opened the door to his daughter's room. Chill followed him inside.

Joan's room was decorated in pink. The curtains, furniture covers, pillows, bedspread, and canopy were all pink gingham. The dressing table, nightstands, and night table were all white maple trimmed in beige. The lampshades were made of the same gingham.

Dr. Morgan took his ophthalmoscope away from Joan's eyes and put it on the bed. He looked up at Tom and Chill. Patty nodded her hello. Her pixie face was drawn, her eyes bright with worry and puzzlement.

Joan had a peaceful expression on her face. She seemed to be sleeping lightly until Chill looked at her more closely. She was obviously deep in slumber. Her breathing was regular, her mouth closed. She was dressed in a nightgown, the covers pulled back, a single sheet rising to her waist. An air conditioner hummed in one window of the room.

"Dr. Morgan, this is Dr. Chillders. I believe you've heard me talk about him and the show we did together. Stan, shake hands with Chill."

The two men shook hands, silently appraising each

27

other. There was a mental squaring-off, a wariness between them. Chill's eyes burned into Morgan's with an intensity that surprised the medical doctor. Yet he felt no hostility from Chillders. Rather, he was almost drawn to him, despite the fact that they held opposing viewpoints. Neither man bothered with the usual amenities. So, in one respect, they understood each other from the beginning. The adversary relationship was almost cordial, and Tom Brunswick was pleased.

"I'm concerned about Joan's condition," Chill said, "both as a friend and for my own reasons."

"Plain enough, Dr. Chillders," Dr. Morgan said. "Let's sit down, shall we?"

"Everyone calls me 'Chill,'" he said, smiling.

Patty seemed relieved that the two men were speaking to each other. She drew Tom and the two men away from Joan's bed, to some chairs arranged near the windows.

"How is she, Stan? Any change?" Tom drew a cigarette from a pack in his shirt pocket, but didn't light it. There were no ashtrays in Joan's room.

"I'm looking for several things here, Tom," Morgan said quietly. "Hysteria. Brain damage. Mental illness, perhaps. No, I'm not saying I suspect any of these things, but I am looking for probable causes of this . . . well, it's probably a type of light coma. There is no swelling of the brain. Her pupils are normal. Her pulse is normal. No sign of shock. No hysterical symptoms. No catatonia."

"What is her state, exactly?" Chill asked.

"I'm puzzled, frankly. *Coma* is not the word I'm looking for to describe her condition. She fainted. she's failed to respond to external stimulation, and she's failed to awaken. She *seems* to be sleeping . . .

28

very peacefully. There were no injuries that I can detect. Her breathing is regular; so is her pulse rate. I checked her last night and treated her for shock. I elevated her legs, listened to her heart, and checked her pulse. This morning, I don't know. It's not a normal situation. At least I've never run across this kind of thing, personally, or in any of my medical reading. Why, do you have a theory?"

"No, no theory. Could the word you're looking for, perhaps, be *trance?*"

"Trance?"

"Instead of *coma.* Could she be in a trance state, as though hypnotized?"

Morgan's eyebrows lifted. He leaned forward, his stethoscope dangling from his neck.

"Why, yes, that's possible. She is in a deep somnolent state, as contrasted to a state of coma. What made you come up with that?"

Chill crossed a leg and looked at Patty and Tom, then back at Dr. Morgan.

"Tom told me what happened. Moses pointed a finger at her. She fainted. It sounds almost as if the old man triggered something in Joan. A prearranged suggestion."

"Hey, wait a minute," said Tom. "You don't mean that Moses has been hypnotizing my daughter?"

"No, I don't mean that at all." Chill seemed to be choosing his words carefully. "I'm thinking that she may have been set up for the fainting, or trance, by a series of external stimuli. These could have been emotionally triggered by what was happening with you and Patty. She may have felt a sudden rush of guilt when Moses pointed the finger at her."

"I think I follow you, Chill," Dr. Morgan said, interested, "but I'd like you to clarify your theory, if you would."

Chill laughed. "Okay, it is a theory, then. What I'm suggesting is that Joan may have been bombarded with a series of impressions: visual, emotional, and/or combinations of stimuli, which made her receptive to a suggestion by Moses that she was responsible for your states of anxiety."

"Fantastic!" breathed Patty.

Dr. Morgan chewed on his lower lip. Tom rolled the unlit cigarette from one side of his mouth to the other.

"Can you prove this?" Dr. Morgan asked. There was no hostility in his question, merely strong professional curiosity.

"Perhaps."

"Do you know hypnosis?" Dr. Morgan asked him.

"I studied clinical hypnosis under Dr. Kroger."

"William Kroger?"

"Yes."

"I'm familiar with his work. He's done quite well in the field of psychosomatic illness."

"Tom, Patty, would you mind letting me talk to your daughter?" Chill asked. "If she's in a kind of hypnotic trance, she may respond to my suggestions."

Tom shot Patty a look. She nodded.

"It's all right with us," Tom said.

"Dr. Morgan?"

"I see no harm in it, as long as the patient shows no signs of being disturbed by your suggestions."

Chill rose from his chair and went to the bed. He looked down at the sleeping girl. He pulled back the sheet. Her pink nightgown flowed over the contours of her body. Tom, Patty, and Dr. Morgan stood on the opposite side of the bed, watching Chill.

"She hasn't eaten or gone to the bathroom since yesterday morning?" Chill asked.

Patty shook her head. She seemed close to tears. Tom drew the cigarette from his mouth. The end of it was soggy. He broke it in two, holding it in his fist. Chill picked up the opthalmoscope and handed it to Dr. Morgan, who stuck it in his back pocket.

"Joan," Chill said softly. "Can you hear me? I know you're asleep, very relaxed. I want you to listen to me. I'm going to help you." He lifted her right hand and smoothed the fingers out. "I want you to move your fingers if you can hear me, Joan. Lift one of your fingers if you can hear my voice."

Patty gasped as Joan lifted her right index finger. Tom started to grin idiotically.

"Very good, Joan. Now, I'm going to have you sleepwalk. You won't get hurt. Your mother will help you. I want you to sit up in bed. Sit up in bed, Joan. You may keep your eyes closed."

Joan began to stir. With an effort, she pulled herself to a sitting position.

"Very good, Joan. Now, we'll help you out of bed." He looked at Patty. "Help me get her up," he told her.

Patty came around to the other side of the bed. She took one of her daughter's arms, Chill the other.

"Stand up, Joan," Chill ordered. The girl rose from the bed. "Your mother's going to take you to the bathroom, Joan. Stand up, now." Joan stood up, her eyes still closed. Her mother led her to the bathroom as the men watched.

"I'll be damned," Tom said.

"It appears, Chill," said Morgan, "that you've made a point."

31

In a few moments, Patty and Joan returned from the bathroom. Patty's face was beaming.

"She went to the bathroom," she exclaimed. "And when I told her what to do, she did it. Chill, you're fabulous!"

Joan came to the bed, a sleepwalker in a pink nightgown.

"Can you awaken her, Chill?" Morgan asked.

"I can try."

"Oh, please, Chill," said Patty. "Wake her up!"

"Be quiet, Patty," Tom said, more tense than ever.

Chill looked at Dr. Morgan.

"With your permission."

Morgan nodded his assent.

Chill took Joan's arm and led her to the bed. He sat her on the edge while the others looked on. He knelt before the girl and took her hands in his.

"Joan. This is Chill. I hope we're friends by now. I'm going to ask you to do something. Take your time. I'm going to count to three. When I say 'wake up,' I want you to open your eyes and wake up. You'll be very rested and relaxed when you wake up. Remember, when I count to three, open your eyes anl wake up. Ready? One, two, three. . . ."

Chill snapped his fingers on the last number.

Joan's eyes moved. The lids fluttered. She stood up, pushing Chill away.

Joan's eyes opened and pierced his with their blind gaze.

There was a distant rumble, and the house shook, the windows rattling. The curtains were moving. The floor seemed to slide underneath their feet.

Joan, still standing, closed her eyes. Chill, struggling to maintain his balance, rushed to her. She drooped in his arms, in a dead swoon.

The far-off rumbling stopped, and the house settled down.

Joan's body turned cold as ice in Chill's arms.

Chill had come to the Brunswicks to celebrate a birthday—would he stay to perform an exorcism?

# CHAPTER FIVE

They lifted the girl back onto the bed.

Dr. Morgan was busy with stethoscope and opthalmoscope. He took her temperature and felt her pulse. Patty drew short breaths. Chill thought she was hyperventilating. He put his arm around her shoulders and patted her arm. As she calmed down, she began to breathe normally. Tom fidgeted with an unlit cigarette, his eyes flicking back and forth from Joan to Dr. Morgan like a tennis fan's.

"Is she all right?" Tom asked.

"Don't know yet," Dr. Morgan said.

Morgan took his time. Tom knew enough by then to keep quiet and wait for the doctor's verdict. Chill observed that Tom was trying hard to control his nervousness.

Joan lay there like a person on a morgue slab. Her face was chalk, her arms and legs rigid. Yet there was a lifelike beauty to her, a haunting aliveness that captured the attention of those who observed her. Her breasts rose and fell with long-spaced, shallow, even breaths. At times, her mother drew a breath as if to help her daughter breathe. The intervals between Joan's breaths became longer and longer, yet there was no sign of struggle, no gasping for air.

Chill watched the girl carefully. He saw that her

breathing had slowed down until it was barely perceptible.

"She's stopped breathing!" Tom gasped.

"No, Tom," Chill said calmly. "She's breathing."

"Instead of fifteen or twenty inhalations a minute, she's dropped down to five," Dr. Morgan said, a note of disbelief in his voice. He felt the girl's forehead. It was dry. There was none of the damp clamminess of shock.

"I—I don't understand," said Patty.

"Neither do I," her husband agreed.

Morgan took Joan's pulse again. He kept moving his two fingers around in the hollow of her wrist. Finally, he found the beating vein and began watching the second hand on his wristwatch.

"How many?" Chill asked, after the doctor had drawn his two fingers away from Joan's wrist.

"Fifty."

"Shouldn't it be seventy something?" Tom asked.

"Seventy-two would be normal. Her breathing's not normal. But she's not in shock." Morgan put his hand up to his forehead.

It was summer but the room had turned chilly. Patty gave a slight shiver, and Tom looked at her oddly. The temperature in the room had dropped.

"What's goin' on here?" Morgan asked, reverting to the colloquial accent that he often tried to conceal. His inflection was tinged with what Northerners called the Southern drawl, but the actual roots of his way of speaking could be traced to New England. Morgan might have been pure Bostonian, circa 1865.

"Look at Joan," Chill said, as he fixed his gaze on the girl.

There was the hint of a smile on Joan's lips as she began to twist on the bed. She drew her legs up

35

toward her stomach. Her head dipped down toward her belly like a flower drooping at eventide. She curled up into a fetal position until her girlish shape was totally obliterated. She had pulled herself into a tight little ball. There was no discernible breathing.

"What's happening to her, doctor?" Patty's voice was tinged with hysteria.

Dr. Morgan said nothing. He leaned over Joan, gently pushed her head back, and pried open an eyelid. The fixed stare was blank, the eye frosty with a dull glaze. He quickly let the lid fall back into place, and Joan reassumed the fetal position. He pulled his hand away as though from a searing flame or from a chunk of dry ice. Chill's eyes narrowed, watching this atypical reaction from an examining physician.

"Stan, what the hell's going on here?" Tom was almost belligerent.

Dr. Morgan shook his head slowly, still looking at his patient.

"Very strange," he said finally. "I can't tell much more until I put an EKG on her and take a cardiogram. Do you want me to arrange for her to be taken to the hospital in Shreveport?"

"No!" Patty exclaimed, startled at her own vehemence.

"Why not?" Dr. Morgan asked.

"Because . . . I want her here. Can't you do anything here?"

"Tom, do you want her here? I'd have to bring in a nurse and haul out equipment. It would be expensive."

"Not as expensive as the hospital," Tom said wryly.

"You've got a point," Dr. Morgan admitted. "I think you'd have a hard time keeping something like this quiet and out of the papers."

"I don't get you, Stan," Tom said.

Dr. Morgan gave Chill a look. He stepped back from the bed and went to the center of the room, where he could see all three of them easily and still keep Joan in view.

"Look, Tom, Patty—I don't know what Joan's got. She seems to be, well, withdrawn . . . regressed, I guess I'm trying to say."

"You mean like a mental case?" Tom scarcely concealed his sarcasm. "A psycho?"

"That's the outward appearance," Morgan admitted, "but that's all I meant. She's not in a coma—not as we know it. Nor," and he looked at Chill when he said this, "is she in a trance state."

"No," said Chill quietly, "I agree."

"Then just what the hell kind of state is she in?" Tom snapped.

"I'd say, offhand," Morgan said carefully, "that Joan's in a state resembling aestivation or hibernation."

"Hiberation?" Tom was incredulous. "You mean like bears?"

"Something like that. Bears are not the only animals that hibernate, however. Many smaller animals lower their body temperatures, adapting their bodies to the winter's lack of heat. They prepare for the long sleep by overeating. Some birds, it is thought, can do the same. Even humans could hibernate and, in fact, perhaps they did at some point in time. I'm just saying that Joan's present state resembles hibernation. I moved to the middle of the room to see if there was a difference in temperature. There is. It's warmer here than by her bed. She happens to be in a cold spot. Her body temperature may have adapted to it, or it

37

could have caused the lowering in temperature. I don't know—is there a draft in here?"

Tom went around the bed, raising and lowering one hand, feeling for drafts.

"There's no draft, but it's cooler there by the bed," he said.

"Exactly. Joan's flesh is ice cold." Morgan's face began to tighten; it was drawn either from worry or confusion. "Anyway, that's my theory right now. I'm interested in what Chill makes of all this. Do you agree with me at all, thus far?"

Chill smiled at Dr. Morgan. His eyes, however, never lost their penetrating hardness. He sensed that he was being tested, that his own credentials were less than acceptable to the medical doctor. He was not being deferred to but being set up for either ridicule or condemnation. It didn't matter. He had confronted medical men before—not skeptics, but men who relied on their degrees and their AMA memberships so much that their minds remained closed to any nonmedical explanation for illness or behavior. Not all medical men were that way, Chill knew, but many were, and he'd learned to be wary not only of those whose minds were closed, but those who were downright hostile. Morgan, he felt, was one of those practitioners who occasionally ventured out from behind the medical books, but drew a line somewhere just short of the inexplicable.

"There are many possible explanations for Joan's condition," Chill replied, "and I'm probably not qualified in your eyes to comment on the medical aspects of her present state. I agree, though, with my limited knowledge, that she appears to be in a state of aestivation. Or . . ."

"Or, what?" Dr. Morgan asked pointedly.

"Or perhaps, through some force, some supernatural cause, she could be in a state of suspended animation."

"Wouldn't that be just another term for the same thing?"

"It could be, but I don't think so in this case," Chill said. "Hibernation, or aestivation, as I understand it, is a state that the organism is prepared for, instinctively and physically. Joan's not fat. In my opinion, she's not hibernating—not willfully, at any rate. Rather, I do think she's in a state of suspended animation. That is, her body does not need to feed on food reserves, stored fat, or protein. She will neither lose nor gain weight. She will continue to live, but will burn so little fuel that the loss to her bodily reserves will be negligible."

"You're talking as though you think she'll be this way for a long time," Patty said gravely.

Chill shrugged.

"What's the matter, Chill, your psychic ability deserting you?" Morgan asked, a trace of contempt in his voice.

"I'm not psychic," said Chill. "At least my psychic ability's not developed much beyond intuition."

Somewhat deflated by Chill's quiet statement, Morgan turned to Tom and Patty.

"I'll have to get on the phone and arrange for nursing and some tests. I still think it would be better if Joan were put into a hospital."

"Just call for what you need, Stan," Tom said. "You can use one of the phones downstairs."

After Tom and the physician left, Patty looked at Chill helplessly.

"It's not good, is it?" she asked.

Chill met her gaze unflinchingly, though he winced inside at her fears.

"No, Patty, it's not good. Your daughter's in the grip of something I can't explain right now."

"You know I don't believe in that stuff. I never did, and I don't now."

"You didn't have to say that, Patty. I know. But I'm staying, if it's all right with you and Tom. I'd like to stay until Joan's well again."

In spite of herself, Patty's sigh of relief filled the room.

# CHAPTER SIX

Kim Michaels swept into the Brunswick living room, a sheaf of papers clutched in her hand. The papers were of different sizes and colors, scraps on which she had scribbled countless phone messages. Kim was a dusky beauty, deeply tanned, with large brown eyes peering out from under a wide, gracefully curved forehead. Her full lips were daubed with a subdued shade of reddish lipstick; her brushed blonde hair was swept back to reveal apple cheeks, a tapered nose with slightly flared nostrils, and a thin, sensuous neck. She was tall—almost 5 feet, 8 inches—and slender, with a model's figure: gentle curves, provocative planes, comely shoulders. She wore an Oriental-print tunic and gabardine slacks.

As soon as Kim entered the room, she began talking, a steady stream of information that made Chill realize once again why Tom Brunswick had chosen her as his administrative assistant.

"You sold the psychic documentary to Brazil and Paraguay—Giannopolous is handling it. Pete Orvis will call from the coast later. Tom, I called everyone on your list and told them the party was cancelled. I reached everyone but the Bransons, uh, Ozzie and Clare and their daughter, Ginger, and I don't know about Chill—" Her gaze drifted from Tom to Chill, who was grinning at her. "Oh, Chill, you devil!" she said, laughing. "You've been here all this time and haven't even said hello to me." Chill got up as she rushed over to him. She threw him off-balance as she squeezed him in an affectionate embrace.

"You were busy," he said. "I haven't been here that long, anyway. I'm glad you are here. Tom and Patty are going to need you."

"How's Joanie?" Kim asked Tom, reluctantly breaking away from Chill.

"Not good, I'm afraid. Dr. Morgan's calling for extra help right now. He's staying in the downstairs bedroom."

"Oh, Tom, I'm sorry," she said, walking over to him. "These messages can wait. You don't want to hear all the shit, do you?"

Tom smiled wearily. He shook his head.

"Let me make us all a drink," Kim said. "Where's Patty? Still upstairs?"

"She's with Joan," Tom said. "I could use a drink. Chill?"

"I brought some juices," he smiled. "They're out in the car. I'll get them."

"Wait, I'll go with you," Kim said. "You can wait a minute for that drink, can't you, Tom?"

"Sure. I'm drained anyway . . . bewildered, I guess. I'd like to sit and gather my thoughts. You run along with Chill and help him get his health foods out of the trunk of his car. I bet you bought out several natural food stores on the way down here, didn't you, Chill?"

"I'll bring you back a vitamin bar to munch on," Chill said. "Maybe then the scotch won't burn up your system so badly."

Tom chuckled, but his heart wasn't in it.

Outside, Kim took Chill's arm.

"What's going on here?" she asked, breathlessly. "Joan's not sick-sick, is she? I mean, it's something else, isn't it? I've never seen Tom so upset, and Patty seemed in a fog when I got here. Young girls like Joanie don't just faint like that. Tom just told me to get on the phone and call all of the people on the guest list and cancel the birthday party. Said he'd called the doctor in Shreveport. I knew enough to keep my mouth shut and make the calls. I talked to Mrs. Ryerson since I couldn't get hold of you. By the way, did you bring Laura Littlefawn with you? Of course you didn't, or she'd be here. Oh, good. I'm selfish. I want you all to myself, Chill," Kim said, looking her seductive best. "Aren't I a bitch? I've missed you, though. Umm, terrible of me to go on like this when Joanie's so sick. What's wrong with her, anyway?"

"Kim, if you'd just shut up for a minute, I'd tell you, dammit!"

They both laughed. Kim squeezed his arm, drawing him close to her. Her scent was subtle, but very feminine. He liked Kim—a lot. She was so open, so childishly ingenuous at times that some people thought her naive. She was not. But she kept that air about her, and Chill found her charming even as he admired her business acumen. "She's soft-tough," Tom had described her once, and Chill had come to realize the accuracy of that statement. Kim was a pussycat, but she had claws. It was to her credit that she seldom had to use them.

"I guess I do talk too much sometimes," she said.

"No, Kim, you just want to know everything at once. Actually, I don't know much myself. Joan's not sick the way we usually think of sickness. You're very

43

perceptive. I think her state has something to do with this house, and with some lingering force here. One doctor would say she's in a coma. Another might say she's catatonic. Now Dr. Morgan thinks she's hibernating."

"Hibernating? Where did Tom get this clown anyway?"

"No, Morgan's sharp enough. Tom trusts him. He'll take care of Joan, I'm sure."

"Sure, but what do you think?"

"I think she's in the grip of something supernatural, Kim. Her system has slowed down to a crawl. She's barely breathing. Somatically, she's sleeping all right. She's in a state of suspension, like a fetus floating in an invisible amniotic sea."

Kim shivered.

"Umm, gives me the willies."

"Patty told you about her experiences?"

Kim nodded.

"Odd, isn't it? Yet Joan was the one who was struck down, not Patty."

"I don't understand."

"Neither do I, Kim—yet." Chill opened the rear door of his station wagon. He picked through some cardboard boxes full of health foods. He handed Kim some bottles of natural apple juice, then sorted through the boxes until he had gathered up raw cashew nuts, sesame sticks, and cheddar crumbles, all in plastic sacks. He stuffed a few carob bars in his pockets.

"What are you going to do?" Kim asked, as Chill followed her up the steps to the front door of the house.

"I'm going to check out the history of this place—

44

talk to Moses and to Patty—and I'm going to get Laura down here to help me out."

Kim stopped short, and Chill bumped into her. She turned and looked up at him with cloudy eyes.

"Chill, did you and Laura ever . . . I mean, did you and she ever get it on together? I always wondered . . . I'm a pushy bitch today, aren't I?"

"Pretty pushy. And, no, Kim—Laura and I've never been to bed together."

"Not yet, you mean."

"Not yet."

Kim let out a long sigh.

"I guess I'm relieved, but I don't know why. She's so beautiful and so eerie, and I know there's something between you two that I can never have. But, still, I hope I can have at least one night with you before she gets here. May I?"

"Is it important to you?"

"Maybe. I'm pretty competitive. You and I have never been to bed either. But we should have—a long time ago."

Chill looked away. He had been attracted to Kim, but they had been thrown together in a working situation before. He hadn't taken advantage of any of the opportunities, and perhaps they both regretted it now.

"Weren't you engaged? Recently?"

"Ha! You know everything, don't you, Chill? Yes, I was engaged. To a louse."

"Movie star, wasn't he?"

"Was. Is. A television bum who dazzled me like he did every woman on the set, from star to script girl. He had a reputation in production companies—he was dangerous on location."

"You knew that from the beginning."

"I did. I was smug enough and secure enough to think I could make him give up his chasing. I was wrong."

"So I'm the rebound guy."

"No, Chill, you're not." Kim blinked away the tears that had started to well up in her eyes. "That's been over for a long time. I just want to see if I have anything left to attract a man."

"Come on, Kim," he said gruffly, pulling her toward the door. "You've got plenty left—everything, in fact."

"Thanks."

They both laughed and went inside the house.

"I'll call Laura tomorrow." Chill said before they went back into the living room. "I do need her here."

"Tomorrow," Kim sighed. "I need you tonight. I've needed you a lot of nights."

"I've missed you, too," he said quietly.

Tom blinked at them as they came into the living room.

"Are we going to have a drink together, or are you two going to run off to the bedroom right now?" he asked drily.

# CHAPTER SEVEN

The old road led away from the Grandier mansion through a thickly wooded area. Chill hadn't even noticed it when he had driven up earlier in the day. It was rutted and full of chuck holes but appeared not to have been used by anything more mechanical than a wagon in some years.

"Moses lives about a quarter of a mile from the house," Tom was saying. "But you'd never know it. The trees and the undergrowth make his place invisible."

"Do you have a phone or intercom to his place?"

"No. Moses is really retired, but we don't tell him that. We inherited him with the place, and I guess he probably wants to live out his last days here. He has nowhere else to go. He gives us a list of groceries once a week. Not much. I think he hunts and fishes for a lot of his food. He keeps the lawn mowed and the brush cleared."

It was mid-afternoon, and they had all managed to have some kind of lunch together. Patty had been so nervous she had eaten little. Kim had picked at the salad Chill had made her, giving him sly glances throughout the meal. Tom had nibbled on a sandwich.

Dr. Morgan drank tea, ate only a hard-boiled egg,

and kept looking at his watch. He had made his phone calls and was waiting for nurses and the equipment to arrive.

Joan's condition had remained static. Mrs. Abigail Dailey, the housekeeper, had helped with lunch, but Chill, a fastidious vegetarian, insisted on preparing his and Kim's meal: a salad of tomatoes, lettuce, celery, mushrooms, and sesame sticks, bathed in Hanes bleu cheese salad dressing; apple juice; and a carob bar for dessert. Kim skipped the carob bar.

Chill had stuck a bunch of sesame sticks in his pocket, and he and Tom went looking for Moses Petitjean, whom Chill was anxious to speak to. Tom was just anxious to get out of the house. He had not yet accepted his daughter's "condition," but he had peremptorily told everyone that he was suspending business until "Joanie's condition cleared up." Chill knew that Tom meant what he said, but Kim would not stop functioning. There were too many important irons in the fire, and Kim would keep things going.

The woods seemed to close in around the two men. The road wasn't straight; it wound through the trees as if uncertain of its destination. Tall pines scratched at the sky, oak and hickory held dominion over the locust and sassafras saplings that fought for a share of the sunlight. Chill could see where Moses had scythed the undergrowth away from the road.

Moses' house stood at the edge of a clearing, surrounded by decades of accumulated junk. Rusted pots; old washing machines, dismembered and disemboweled; three gutted hulls of ancient automobiles, oxidized to a featureless brown; tin cans and plastic jugs; twisted bedsprings; galvanized washtubs bent into shapeless chunks of metal; parts of garden tools and scraps of lumber; burst batteries, their plates buckled and fluids dehydrated; broken jars; strips of twisted and nail-gored aluminum; and frayed, rotten ropes. A thousand and one discarded artifacts of civilization were scattered and heaped outside the cabin, a haven for a half-dozen scrawny cats of various hues and sizes, for bone-gaunt hounds with big ears and rheumy eyes, for dirt-wallowing chickens, for lizards, snakes and rats. A battered Ford pickup stood off to the side, almost regal in its haughty stance at the end of the road they had followed from the mansion. The truck was obviously in running condition, since the marks of its tire treads were still fresh in the slightly damp earth near the house. So the old road was in use.

Chill noticed the cistern, hanging incongruously over one side of the house. It wasn't really hanging, of course, but was supported by a wooden frame that was concealed by climbing vine. Despite its age, the shack was not as ramshackle as he would have suspected. The porch, like Thoreau's cabin, held only two chairs, one a rocker, the other straight-backed with a cane seat. Coffee cans, with tired plants struggling for life in dessicated depths, crowded one corner of the porch. A refrigerator and two tall butane tanks were ballast on the other end. The screen door gleamed with new wire patches. Flies clung to the screen like winged leeches, peering bug-eyed inside.

"It's a mess, isn't it?" Tom remarked. "Like something out of Ma and Pa Kettle."

"Looks lived in," Chill said, smiling.

"I'll introduce you to Moses and then go on back so you two can talk."

"Fine."

The two men walked up onto the porch. A mourning dove cooed from somewhere behind the house. None of the hounds moved.

"Moses?" Tom called through the screen door. The flies buzzed against it in anticipation.

"You all come in," Moses replied, from somewhere inside the house.

Tom opened the door, and a dozen flies soared through the gap. Tom and Chill went inside, the spring on the door banging it shut behind them.

The inside of the house contrasted sharply with the outside. The linoleum floor was freshly scrubbed, the aroma of Lysol clinging to the faded pattern. Other alien smells fought for recognition. The neatness inside was immediately apparent. Although the place was crammed with objects, they all seemed to be in their respective places. There were lamps and chairs and tables, and a couch in the living room, which was divided from the kitchen by a half-wall. Religious pictures in cheap frames adorned the walls, which were covered with cheap wallpaper. An oilcloth, patchy but clean, covered the round table in the kitchen. Strips of fly ribbon hung strategically from the ceiling. The visible kitchen utensils were clean and stacked where they belonged, on the stove, the counter, the wall.

Moses shuffled out of a bedroom adjoining the living room. His overalls were clean and freshly pressed. Because he was hatless, his white hair seemed sparse and brittle on his skull. He came through the parted curtains like a shadow, his eyes big and bright as though he had been sipping wine.

"Mistah Bruns'ick," he said, nodding his head, "won'tcha take you'uns a chair?"

"Thanks, Moses, I can't stay," said Tom. "I wanted

you to meet a friend of mine. He wants to talk to you, if you don't mind."

"Sho, Mistah Bruns'ick, I'se pleased to meet your fren'."

"Moses, this is Dr. Chillders."

"Doctah? You mus' be hear 'bout Miz Joanie."

"Call me Chill, Moses, and yes, I'm here about Joan, but I'm not that kind of doctor."

Moses' accent was what Chill would have described as "deep Southern." The black man had a lazy, comfortable drawl that Chill soon got used to since it differed only slightly from the Georgia backwoods dialects that he recognized.

The black man drew his head backward and to the side, eyeing Chill with surprised wariness.

"What kind of doctah is you?"

Chill laughed.

"I'm a doctor of philosophy, Moses."

"I sees," said Moses. "You gentlemans like some chicory, somethin' to drink?"

"I've got to be running along, Moses," Tom said, shaking his head. "I'll see you later, Chill."

The two men watched Tom leave. The screen door banged shut, but not before a small cloud of flies took advantage of the opened door and entered the kitchen. Tom's footsteps clattered across the porch, then faded away in the yard.

Moses lifted his eyebrows.

"Nothing for me, thanks. I'll just munch on these." Chill drew a cellophane bag of sesame sticks from his pocket and held it out to Moses.

"What is they?"

"Sesame sticks. Kind of like pretzels."

"Sho' enough?" Moses took a couple of sticks from the sack.

"Can we sit down?" Chill asked.

Moses ambled to a chair, as Chill sat on the couch.

"Mighty tasty."

"I wonder if you'd mind answering some questions," Chill said.

"What kinda questions?"

"About Joan. About this place here."

Moses' eyes narrowed slightly. He began to massage one hand with the other. The knuckles were knotted with arthritis, the fingers long and bony.

"Go ahead," he said curtly.

"Thanks, Moses. I'm trying to help, you know."

"They's some things better left alone."

"You're probably right. I won't take up much of your time. I'm curious about why you think Joan was the cause of the odd happenings around here."

"Who told you that?"

"Her mother indicated to me that you had as much as accused Joan of being responsible for her mother's strange experiences."

Moses leaned back in his chair and slapped a bony hand on his knee.

"Whooie! That woman sho do have an imagination! She take on some. That woman touched in the head."

Chill knew he was lying. Moses' eyes were everywhere, except on Chill's. And they were filled with fear.

"What did you mean when you pointed at Joan and told her parents to ask *her* what was going on?"

Moses' eyes widened, and he continued to avoid Chill's steady, penetrating stare. He could find no place to hide his hands. They hung on the ends of his arms like chunks of rope.

"Mistah, you steppin' into somethin' mighty bad

52

here. It ain't good to mess with things you can't understand."

"Let me try, Moses. Maybe you misjudge me."

Moses' eyes narrowed, and he looked intently at Chill for the first time. He reached into a pocket of his overalls and pulled out a can of Red Seal. He opened the lid and dipped bony fingers into the mass of tobacco. He stuffed a wad of it next to his lower gum and worked the tobacco backward with his tongue, shaping it up into a moist ball.

"I'se been on this place a long time. Seen many things. Now, I don't know these folks what are living here now, but Mrs. Bruns'ick, she be kin to the Grandiers. They all dead, 'ceptin' her. And her daughter—Joan. She's more like them than her ma. Spittin' image."

"Like the Grandiers? What were they like?"

"Good folks. Treated me just fine. Kept to theirselfs. Born, died, and buried here."

"Buried here? Where?"

Moses eyed Chill suspiciously.

"What you mean to do?" he asked.

"Why, nothing, really. I just wondered where the family plots were. Tom didn't mention a graveyard."

"They's one."

"Do you have any children, Moses?" Chill said, abruptly changing the direction of the questioning.

"Me'n my missus had a girl. We called her Wilma after my wife's mother. She run off young."

"How young?"

"About seven, I reckons. Just up and took off somewheres. Never did find her."

"You mean she got lost?"

"Some said lost; some said kidnap. I don't rightly know."

53

"What about the Grandiers? Are they buried in the cemetery?" He was back to the main question.

"Some is. Not the old folks though, them as what just died. They in a tomb."

"Well, will you take me there?"

Moses' eyes widened until the whites dwarfed the pupils.

"I don't go near that place—no, sir!"

"Well, just tell me where it is, then."

Moses stood up.

"Over in the bluffs, but it's all overgrowed now. Hard to find, and if you did find it . . ."

"Yes?"

Moses turned away.

"It's haunted," he said, his voice barely audible.

Chill got up and followed Moses into the kitchen. His nose sniffed for the alien smell he was trying to sort out from the disinfectant.

"How is it haunted?" he persisted.

"You better get on back up to the main house, doctor. I got no more to say."

Chill reached for the black man's sleeve and touched it. His hand closed around Moses' arm.

Moses turned, surprised. The lump in his cheek seemed to grow, to throb as he worked his teeth back and forth slowly.

"I—I want us to be friends," Chill said. "I want you to trust me. I'm here to help."

Chill could feel the tension in the old man's arm. His muscle was like a coiled spring, ready to snap.

The black man's eyes teared, welling up with a sadness that touched Chill. He opened his mouth to speak, but no words came. He looked around him, as if in fear. He put a hand on Chill's and shook his head.

"I just can't say no more, Dr. Chlllders. I just can't."

Chill nodded in understanding. It was obvious that Moses was terrified.

"Some other time, Moses."

"Yes sir. That'd be just fine. Some other time." Moses was obviously relieved. Chill released his grip on the man's arm. Chill wanted to speak some words of comfort to Moses, but knew that this wouldn't be proper. The black man had a lot of pride. It was probably all that he had left. Chill didn't want to be the one to damage it.

"We'll talk again, Moses," he said, going toward the door. Chill looked around the room once more, making a mental note of the clean but shabby mismatched furniture, and of an old double-barreled shotgun leaning against the wall in one corner of the room. "Thanks for your help. I'll find the tomb on my own."

He could hear Moses sucking in his breath.

Chill started for the door, but a cough from Moses brought him up short. He turned and looked at the old man, his eyebrows raised in query.

"Be better you don't go near that ol' tomb out there," Moses said quietly. "Ol' man Grandier, he done put a curse on it. Ain't nobody supposed to go out yonder—no sir."

"Is that what you think happened to Joan?"

Moses shook his head.

"I don't know, sir, but she out thataway."

"What kind of curse was it, do you know?"

"No, sir, I just knows that ol' man Grandier didn't want nobody snooping around his grave."

"Thanks, Moses. You've been a big help."

Chill opened the screen door. He batted at the flies that streamed past him. Just as he stepped outside, the alien smell that had eluded him struck a responsive chord in his mind. He stopped, as the screen door banged closed behind him.

"Uh, one more thing, Moses," he said. "Do you smoke?"

"No, sir. I just dips snuff now and again."

"Didn't think so. Bad for the lungs. Thanks for your time. I'll be seeing you."

"Yes, sir," Moses said, invisible behind the swarming screen. Chill detected the slight tremble in the man's voice.

Chill walked back down the road, conscious of at least one pair of eyes on him. Perhaps two.

The smell he had detected in Moses' house was strong. Rank. It only could have come from a cigar.

And Moses just told him he didn't smoke.

# CHAPTER EIGHT

Ozzie Branson watched his daughter, Ginger, with veiled eyes. She had dark hair like her mother, but her pug nose was just like his. Ozzie knew things that Clare, his wife, wouldn't accept—couldn't accept.

Ginger was 19, and she had a monstrous crush on Tom Brunswick.

Ozzie's stomach twisted in the grips of a private anguish, aided and abetted by the gin in his martini. Ginger was coming on strong with Tom, knowing that Patty was upstairs with their daughter, who was in some kind of coma. Clare was babbling on with Kim, oblivious to Ginger's open invitation to Tom. And Kim didn't notice because her back was turned. Clare was swilling her drink, and Ozzie knew that, as usual, she had fortified herself before they had left the house. To make matters worse, their visit to the Brunswick house had turned into a nightmare.

For the past half-hour, men and equipment had been coming in and out the front door. It was ominous, positively ominous. Tom had told them very little, miffed at being told by Dr. Morgan that he was in the way. So they had sat here sloshing down the drinks until Clare was half in the bag and Ginger, shamelessly, was moving in on Tom like a bird of prey. Yet to reprimand her would draw attention to the problem. Ginger was coy, rather than aggressive, even though Ozzie could see that her very coyness was a veiled assault on Tom's ego and his masculinity.

He took another sip of his martini. Perhaps he was reading it all wrong, but he didn't think so. Tom was alight with the attention he was getting from Ginger. Maybe he needed that now, with his daughter so ill and the party plans spoiled, the house in a turmoil. Maybe he needed a young woman's attentions just as he, Ozzie, needed this martini to dull his anger at both his wife and daughter.

*Maybe*, he thought, *it's none of my business. Live and let live.*

He ambled away from the bar, away from his thoughts. Not toward Ginger and Tom, but toward his wife and Kim. He felt he was an outsider with either couple, but on surer ground with the pragmatic Kim and his giddy wife.

"About time you joined us," Clare said. "Kim's been telling me all about the big mystery here."

Clare Branson was an ostentatious woman in her early forties, well-preserved, if one didn't look too closely at her restless, sad eyes and at the lines on her face, which she fought to iron out with energetic movements. Her Clairol-blonde hair was exquisitely coiffed, none of the dark roots showing, and her makeup might have made a Max Factor jealous. There was just enough of it, and it allowed the light to enhance her attractive features, although, again, one ought not to look too closely at the texture under the pancake. Her figure was still slender and her tummy rounded just so from careful dieting. She wore dark green slacks, with a green and white checked silk blouse. Her breasts were small and pointed in the expensive bra she wore. Her fingernails were carefully manicured, her hands long and sleek as she gestured animatedly, calling attention to them rather than to her face. Her eyes were a cold, vacuous blue, toned up by thick false eyelashes that kept batting over them like automatic shutters.

"And what is the mystery?" Ozzie asked casually, running his fingers through his sandy-colored hair. "Or are you talking about Joan's illness?"

"Well, of course I'm talking about Joan's illness, silly man, but the fact is that the famous Dr. Russell V. Chillders—you know, the man that Tom had on his television program—is here to investigate the mysterious forces of this house. I don't mean to be offhanded about Joan's coma, or whatever it is, but I think it's fascinating that the mystery man himself is trying to find out what's causing it. Kim says that Dr. Chillders thinks there's some supernatural connection. Don't you find that utterly fascinating?"

Kim looked ashamed.

"I don't know much about this Dr. Chillders," Ozzie said, "but I'm sure there's some rational explanation for Joan's illness. She probably got a bug or something. Why don't they take her to a hospital?"

"Tom thinks she'd get better care here. Patty does too. If you'd seen Joan, I think you'd agree that it's not something ordinary that she has."

"Maybe she fell, hit her head . . ." Ozzie said feebly.

"Oh, Ozzie, come on, don't be such a party pooper," his wife chided. "You're always so practical. You know this place has always had an odd reputation. I mean, when the Grandiers were alive and living here, there was a lot of talk about them and their standoffish ways. I've always wondered about them."

Ozzie looked pleadingly at Kim.

"Clare's always looking for trouble," he explained. "She and this Chillders ought to get along. She sees dark forces at work in the most ordinary situations and circumstances. The Grandiers were old, and they lived quietly. I see nothing mysterious about that. Patty inherited the property, and now Clare's sure that there is a curse on the place. Isn't that right, Clare?"

"Oh, you," Clare huffed. "I thought you'd be that way." She turned to Kim. "That's an attorney for you. Ozzie wants nothing but the facts, ma'am, always the facts. Well, there are a lot of things in this world that can't be explained, Ozzie dear, at least not by your legalistic reasoning!"

"I know, Clare," Ozzie said drily, "and you're one of them." His smile showed her that he was teasing, but Clare was only slightly mollified. She sipped long at her drink and pretended to pout.

Kim stood up.

"Here's Chill now," she said.

Clare almost gagged on an ice cube. She began to straighten her clothes, tapping at her hair with a single slender finger.

Chill walked into the room and, noticing the intimate twosome, gave Tom a stern glance and nodded at Ginger, who seemed to resent his intrusion. Her drive for attention had been temporarily halted.

"I guess it's time for introductions," Tom said, rising and self-consciously pulling at his clothes. He read Chill's silent admonition and raised his glass.

"Straight ginger ale," he explained. "Chill, this is Ginger Branson, daughter of my friends over here. Ozzie, Clare, shake hands with Russell Chillders."

The circumstances hardly called for gaiety, and Kim could detect Chill's resentment at the seemingly happy-go-lucky gathering. But he was too much the gentleman and the diplomat to say anything.

"I've heard some fascinating things about you, Dr. Chillders," Clare was saying.

"Chill, please."

"Tell me, what do *you* think is wrong with Joan?"

"I have no idea," Chill said.

"Oh, come now," said Ozzie. "Surely you have some theory. Joan was a perfectly normal, healthy girl. I mean until this happened. I don't like speaking of her in the past tense of course, but Tom filled me in."

"It's just tragic," Clare put in.

"I'm sure Dr. Morgan will tell us more when he can," Chill said.

"Yes," Tom said quickly, "Dr. Morgan's handling things. Chill is my guest."

"I want to talk to you, Tom," Chill said, his eyes flashing a sense of urgency. His direct gaze shut out the others so that they knew they were excluded from eavesdropping.

"Why, sure, Chill. What's up? Can we talk about it here?" Tom looked wistfully at Ginger.

"No, I'm afraid not. I hope your other guests will forgive me. It's rather important."

"Ah, yeah, okay. Ozzie, Clare, Ginger—be right back. Just relax. Kim knows where everything is. Sorry about all this."

There was silence among the others as the two men left the room. Tom seemed to be trying to draw himself up to greater height, to throw off the effects of the alcohol and the pills. Beside Chill, he seemed to be almost shambling in the wake of the taller man's purposeful stride.

When they were alone, Chill took his friend's shoulders in his hands and looked at him intently.

"Tom," he said, "I'm talking to you as a friend. I don't know what you've got going with that girl in there, but your timing's way off. You've got a sick daughter upstairs, a worried wife, and you don't need any complications."

"Hey, Chill, I was just—maybe you're right. A pretty girl gives you a smile, and you get carried away and forget who you are. I guess I was just trying to escape and wipe all this out of my mind. Thanks."

They stood outside the door, out of sight and earshot of the others. The foyer was deserted.

"I'm worried, too, about all the booze you're taking on—mixing that with the medication you're taking. If you're not careful, Dr. Morgan will have two patients upstairs."

Tom shook his head groggily.

"I—I'm sorry. I just can't seem to calm down. I feel rotten about Joanie and so damned helpless. God, Chill, what did we do to deserve this?"

Chill could see that Tom was close to breaking down. He could feel the man's shoulders trembling in his grip.

"It's not anyone's fault. Look, Tom, just what are those people doing here? The Bransons. Do they think they're still at a party?"

"I invited Ozzie and his family for Joan's birthday party. Kim tried to cancel, but they were off somewhere. She couldn't reach them. Ozzie's an attorney in New Orleans."

"Well, they don't belong here at a time like this. Their daughter, Ginger—is that her name? Well, she had a man-hungry look in her eyes. If Patty saw her coming on like that, she'd be furious—and with good reason."

"Aw, hell, Chill, everything's mixed up. I don't know what I'm doing. I encouraged the girl. It took my mind off—off the other stuff."

"Okay, well, keep your mind on the other stuff. It's the only way you're going to stay together. By the way, I talked to Moses. He knows a lot more than he's telling."

"Oh? I'm not surprised. He's something of a sneak, I think. You never hear him walk up behind you, but he always pops up out of nowhere."

"Look, Tom, is there anyone else staying in that shack with him?"

Tom looked surprised.

"Why, no. There shouldn't be. Moses has no family that I know of. He lives alone."

"Maybe," Chill said thoughtfully.

Suddenly there was a commotion upstairs. Tom and Chill both looked up.

"What's going on?" Tom asked.

There were muffled shouts, the clatter of falling furniture, and a heavy thud.

"Let's get up there!" Chill barked, striding across the foyer. Both men hit the stairs running, bounding up them two at a time. When they reached the upper level, the door to Joan's room burst open. An hysterical Patty rushed out, babbling incoherently. Chill grabbed her in his arms as Tom braked to a halt.

"Good Lord, Patty, what's the matter?" her husband asked.

"Oh, Tom, it's horrible, horrible. . . ." She pulled herself free from Chill's arms and clutched at her husband. He put his arms around her and drew her close to him.

Dr. Morgan and one of the nurses he'd hired came

63

through the doorway. Chill raised his eyebrows questioningly. Morgan ignored him.

"The nurse will have to take care of Mrs. Brunswick. She's hysterical. Mrs. Baines, please."

"Hey, Morgan," Tom said testily, "do you mind explaining all this? My wife's upset, and I want to know why!"

"Baines!" Dr. Morgan helped separate Tom and Patty. The nurse, a chunky woman in her mid-forties, expertly led Patty away from the group. The woman's face was slightly pockmarked, the depressions filled in with pancake makeup, giving her face a pasty look. Her red hair was tied up in a bun under a nurse's cap.

"Come in here, gentlemen, and I'll show you why Mrs. Brunswick is upset."

Chill and Tom followed Morgan into Joan's room. The doctor closed the door. Another nurse, younger than Baines, stood next to the girl's bed. The sharp antiseptic aroma of alcohol permeated the room. The fumes stung their nostrils and caused a slight tearing in their eyes.

The nurse was bathing Joan's feet in the clear liquid.

"Hold it up a minute, Miss Arnold," Dr. Morgan ordered.

Chill looked at the nurse carefully. She seemed to be puzzled about something. She was in her late twenties or early thirties, with long, dark hair and green eyes that seemed vacuous and unable to focus. Her lips were wide and thin, trembling slightly.

"This is what upset your wife, Tom," Dr. Morgan said, tracing his finger around one of Joan's heels. "Her feet were covered with this when we first no-

64

ticed it. Look at the floor underneath the bed—the posts at this end."

Tom and Chill stared at the dark green substance that outlined the girl's heel, that flowed in rivulets up from the floor and along the bedposts and over the sheets.

"What the hell is it?" There was more than bewilderment in Tom's voice. There was fear, too.

"I don't know," Dr. Morgan said flatly. "A fungus. Some kind of mold."

Chill looked around the room. A bottle of dextrose solution lay shattered a few feet from the bed, a rubber tube dangling from its dismembered mouth. The stand was leaning against the wall, two of its wheels in the air, wedged against the table where the electrocardiograph sat, without current, its plug dangling a few inches from the floor. Isolyte fluid seeped into the carpeting, its stain spreading like liquid on a blotter.

"Continue with the alcohol," Dr. Morgan told the nurse.

"Patty do all this?" Chill asked quietly. The nurse coughed and lowered her head.

Dr. Morgan nodded.

"Why?" asked Tom.

"She saw me taking a sample of the fungus and scraping it into a plastic bag for analysis. It was too much for her." Morgan's tone was almost apologetic. It was obvious to Chill that he too was unsettled by the strange growth.

"Have you ever seen anything like this before, doctor?"

Chill moved closer to the bed, avoiding eye contact with Dr. Morgan.

"Not on a living person, no," Dr. Morgan said. His

voice was muffled, as though he had an obstruction in his throat.

"What the hell's that supposed to mean?" Tom snapped.

"Let it go, Tom," Chill said evenly. His tone brought Tom up short. He clamped down on his next words, and swallowed them. He watched Chill, who was staring down at Joan with a puzzled expression on his face.

The girl was no longer curled up in a fetal position. She was lying on her back, her legs spread wide. The sheet, covering only her torso, clung to her body, revealing its sensuous contours. There was a trace of a smile on her face. Her eyes were still closed. She looked, thought Chill, like a woman who was waiting for her lover—or dreaming about sex.

# CHAPTER NINE

At first there was darkness.

There was no pain.

Then, some light again. Cold, sterile—steady just behind her eyes. Yet she was not cold. It was only an impression of coolness—from the pale light. It was like a winter dawn, hovering on the brink of darkness, hesitant, unwavering.

She tried to remember.

Nothing. No, something.

Moses' finger, pointing at her. Then, a snap! As though a cord had been stretched tight, then broken.

The darkness smothered her senses. She had been aware of that sensation. The others, too. It was like falling through oil. A slow sinking through layers of darkness, a feeling of weightlessness, of suspension in a thick and invisible liquid.

Voices filtered through the gauzy light of her mind. Unintelligible sounds—faint, foreign. The light held steady, dim, admitting only the few sounds.

She began to feel the light's comfort, yet there was still no warmth—only a promise of safety in its faint glow.

She felt safe in the darkness, too. In the suspension—that floating, as in amniotic fluid.

*A thought slipped into her mind she was being born—again.*

*Born again!*

*It was like that. There was quiet and peace once more. There was security, enough light to let her know that she was alive, enough dark to . . .*

*She was aware of the voices, between moments of serenity and feeling lost. They drifted in through the dark. They floated through the spare light and pinged against her inner ear, tinny, tiny. From far away, little pinpoints of garbled sound. Needles stippling the dark, perforating the black space like a host of diminutive stars until they took on light of their own. They still sounded tinny, though, even if she could understand the words, as if she was hearing them underwater.*

*She knew her ears must be plugged up, because the sounds that filtered through to her brain were like dead stones falling on a tin roof. Her brain felt numb. . . .*

Dr. Morgan tapped Joan's right wrist with the percussion hammer. The wrist jerked spasmodically. Chill and Tom stood at the edge of the bed, near the foot, watching him. Francine Arnold, who was sitting in a chair reading a paperback novel, was on duty.

Dr. Morgan lifted the sheet and raised Joan's right knee slightly. He tapped behind the knee with the hard red rubber hammer, holding it by its stainless steel handle. The reflex muscle responded. Joan's knee jerked perceptibly as the tendon stretched.

"Her reflexes are normal." Dr. Morgan looked at the screen on the monitor beside the bed, a continuous electroencephalograph reading blipping across the green expanse. "She's suffered no brain damage, no trauma that I can detect. She's not in a coma. If she were, I'd have to insist that she be taken to the hospital immediately."

Morgan squeezed her Achilles tendon between two fingers. There was, again, visible reflex action. He placed her leg back alongside the other and drew the sheet back over the girl's limbs. Patty had dressed her in a simple gown. Her arms were outstretched at her sides, intravenous needles buried in her veins, taped to her skin. Isolyte fluids dripped steadily down the tubes, moving along the transparent lines like a steady procession of crystal beads.

"Miss Arnold," Morgan said to the nurse, whose head popped up out of her book. "I want you to keep a close watch on Miss Brunswick's temp and BP and chart it all." The nurse closed her book and set it on the floor underneath her chair. She stood up and took a notebook from Joan's nightstand. She handed it to Dr. Morgan, a slight flash of defiance in her greenish eyes. Morgan didn't notice it.

"Why do you have those tubes in Joan?" Tom asked, still slightly bewildered over all the equipment at his daughter's bedside.

"We've got to maintain homeostasis," Morgan said, glancing through the nurse's careful notes. "She's getting I.V. to keep her stable—saline and potassium. I've taken urine samples and sent them to Shreveport for electrolyte tests. I may have to add daily serum electrolytes and will check her magnesium levels daily as well. I'm also, in the other arm there"—he pointed to the other hanging bottle—"putting in dextrose. That's all the nourishment she's getting. Her EEG looks good, though. It's not flattening out. Her brain is getting plenty of oxygen despite her deep sleep."

"What the hell's wrong with her, Stan?" Tom's eyes

were wide, and he seemed to be staring beyond Morgan.

"I think," Morgan said quietly, "that Chill here may have come closest to a diagnosis, after all. Your daughter's not ill—not in any clinical sense that I can determine. She's in some kind of stabilized suspension of normal bodily functions. Her heart and pulse are good, steady even at their slowed-down rate. Her brain is functioning. She's in some kind of abnormally caused deep sleep. If I thought any different, I'd override your objections and take her to the hospital immediately. This is irregular, as it is, but I'm confident that she could get no better treatment than she's now getting. She's absorbing the I.V. nourishment, her color's good, and she's breathing fine, although at a slower than normal rate. Her blood pressure is low, but that's in keeping with the other aspects of this 'suspended' state."

"Are you worried about her, doctor?" Chill asked.

"In a way, I suppose, Dr. Chillders. I'm at a loss to explain her condition medically, at least in human terms. It's an oddity. But I am encouraged by her EEG, her EKG, which I took earlier, and by her stable condition. She's slowed down, as if she were in *hibernation*, and I think she'll come out of it. She's not in shock, but you'll notice we have her legs slightly elevated just in case. I'm only worried that she will sink so far into sleep that she will go into a comatose state."

"That would be dangerous?" Tom asked.

"I think so. We don't fully understand coma. We know what it looks like, but we are really helpless to do anything but maintain a patient in homeostasis through drugs and I.V. nutrients and vital minerals."

70

"She looks peaceful enough," Tom said blankly.

"Well, from all I can determine, Tom," Dr. Morgan said, "she's just asleep, not sick."

"What about that mold that was on her feet?" Chill asked.

Morgan looked away, snapping the notebook closed.

"I can't explain that," he said.

Chill's eyes narrowed.

"Come on, Tom, there's nothing we can do here. You've got to eat and get some rest." Chill took Tom's arm and started to lead him away from the bed. "Thank you, Dr. Morgan," he said, walking Tom toward the door. "We know she's in good hands."

Morgan stood for a long time, looking at the floor after the two men left. He wondered if Chill was right. He hoped so, but he was uncertain.

"Thanks, Miss Arnold," he told the nurse. "You've done well on this chart. Wake Mrs. Baines at midnight, and call me when you come on in the morning. You know where my room is."

"Yes, doctor, of course," said Miss Arnold.

Like a distant thunderstorm, the oscillograph beam blipped across the screen in mildly flaring patterns.

Morgan looked at it for a long moment, then left the room.

Nurse Arnold closed the door to Joan's room and went back to sit beside the bed. She glanced once at the oscillograph, shrugged, and then picked up her paperback book. It was a romance about a nurse. She crossed her legs and began reading where she'd left off. She didn't notice the frenzied beam on the scope. It was dancing like the aurora borealis, the lights covering the screen with urgent and violent zigzags.

*Her brain came awake. Jolted out of its dormancy—but the light. It stabbed at her cortex, beamed into the cerebellum, flowed through the brainstem. She could almost see her brain, a cauliflower of energy pulsating in her skull. She knew her eyes were closed, but she could see the room she was in. No, she could sense it. That was important, she knew. In a way, she felt more alive than she ever had. It was as if her eyelids had become thin so that she could see through them.*

*The room was dim; night clutched at the windows—night, and something else. Something sentient, covert, furtive. Something with the sheen of a color on its surface. A color like green, burning fluorescent in the moonlight.*

*There was a thought forming in her mind. She didn't struggle to define it clearly. She just waited for it to form. The peacefulness was still with her, the tranquility like a warm stone in the center of her pool of being.*

*Alien.*

*That was the word she made from the thought.*

*But who? Herself? The other person in the room? Who was the alien?*

*Pain in her arms. Distant, but evident. Sustenance entering her veins. She didn't need it. She knew that. Maybe that was the "alien." No, it was something else. The person in the room? Herself? Her thought was all tangled up, confused. There was no way to move her arms. It was as if her brain were detached from her body. Yet she could feel the strength in her sleeping self. An anticipation—as if she was waiting for someone, or something. Waiting for something to happen.*

*Another thought intruded.*

*Don't think!*

*Then, another.*

*Wait!*

These messages were strong signals that sparked from one neuron to another, brilliant, quick impulses that flashed through the axon to the dendrites and cell bodies of other neurons. Strangely enough, in some reason she understood this. She could almost see it happening. She could picture the nerve impulses transmitting their chemical messages to parts of her brain. She also knew that she was activating the EEG while floating in muscular atonia. Cells were sleeping; others were awake. She might have been dreaming, should have been dreaming, except that the dream state was real. She knew that the other person in the room was reading, that there were bottles hung over her bed and fluids dripping into her veins.

Something else, too elusive to grasp, clawed at her brain.

She felt split in two.

Part of herself was pulled toward the window, toward the outside world. The other half of her being was pulled toward the bed and the house. She was suddenly gripped with a sense of isolation, stronger than before. She felt another fragment of herself spiraling upward and backward through space, a cluster of neurons returning to other neurons somewhere back in time. She could see them break loose, see the energy in them pulsating, searching for a destination, see their sparks reaching out to make positive contact, silver penises searching for a lost womb.

A longing stirred in her body. This was an ancient ache that cried out for remembrance. The lights in her head danced away out of sight, and she forgot

73

about them. They were like spaceships sent out to cold, faraway worlds.

She saw herself split in two, a Janus brain that had two faces, two compulsions.

She felt her legs spread wide.

Then the longing became attached to a name:

Iscaaron.

# CHAPTER TEN

Mrs. Abigail Dailey, the Brunswicks' just-past-middle-aged cook, had cleared off the supper dishes and was pouring fresh coffee into the guests' cups. The woman moved quickly but stiffly, her arthritic joints restricting her movements. Her thin lips were clenched tightly together as she tried to ignore the pain in her elbow while she poured the coffee. Her eyes were dulled by the pain even though she'd just taken two buffered aspirin. She looked forward to taking off her girdle and letting her hair down out of its tight bun.

"Your arm bothering you again?" Patty asked, concerned.

"Not only my arms, but my knees and feet," Mrs. Dailey said. There was no hint of bitterness in her voice, yet she did not smile.

"Better leave the dishes," Patty said. "I can get them later."

"No, it's my job," said the cook, as she passed by Chill's chair. He held a hand over his cup.

"I made some herb tea," he said, pointing to a steaming pot.

"Don't be silly, Abbie," Tom said.

Abbie frowned at Chill.

"I need to do something anyway," Patty said. "Please—"

"Oh, don't fuss about me so," said Mrs. Dailey. "I'll just toddle off to bed in a while. I hope your daughter's better in the morning."

"I'm sure she will be," Patty said tightly, her face drawn and pasty. Tom put his hand on his wife's for reassurance. The Bransons, who would be staying overnight, exchanged looks. Dr. Morgan avoided looking at the Brunswicks, attending to his napkin, which had begun to slip off his lap. Suddenly, Ginger rose from the table.

"May I be excused?" she asked, looking at her mother.

Clare Branson nodded at her daughter.

Ginger gave Tom a wistful look that he didn't catch. She glanced at Chill, whose eyes were hard on hers, shrugged, and pushed her chair away from the table and stood up.

"Good night, everyone," the girl said.

A chorus of "good nights" followed her out of the dining room.

No one spoke for several seconds.

"She *will* be all right, won't she, Stan?" Patty pleaded.

Morgan took a sip of his coffee, blowing at the liquid before he put the cup to his lips.

"I don't foresee any further complications tonight," he said. "We'll see how she is in the morning. She's getting the best of care, under the circumstances."

"Brandy, anyone?" Tom asked, with little conviction in his voice.

"No, Tom, I think you've done enough drinking for today," Patty said.

"Sure, Patty, you're right. I was just offering our guests . . ."

Kim Michaels looked at Chill, her eyebrows drawn together. She had been silent throughout most of the meal and, like Patty, had only picked at her food. Chill, too, had been reticent during supper, as though he was saving his conversation for later, which was, indeed, the case.

"Patty, I'd like to know more about your family, the Grandiers," Chill said, when the silence was almost intolerable. "Did you know much about them?"

"Not much," Patty said with a sigh, as if happy to turn her mind to something other than worry over Joan. "Bernard Grandier, my great-uncle, was pretty antisocial from what I've heard. I scarcely knew him. That's why Tom and I were so surprised to learn that we'd inherited this place. We thought it'd be fun to live here. I used to try to get my folks to tell me stories about Uncle Bernard, but they were never much help. My father, Norman Grandier, thought Uncle Bernard was strange, and my mother, Ida, wouldn't have anything to do with him. Uncle Bernard never had any children, so far as I know. I heard some talk from the neighbors after we moved here—I mean, about how weird the Grandiers were—but not in those terms. Mainly, I guess I used my intuition to fill in the blank spaces. No one in this region ever said much about the Grandiers, except that they kept to themselves, they paid their bills—things like that."

"How did you feel about his death?"

"I didn't feel anything much. I tried to see the attorney who handled the estate for my great-uncle, but he had disappeared."

"Disappeared?" Chill's eyes grew hard.

"Well, he had moved. I couldn't locate him."

"What was his name?"

"Pierre Duchamps. We only saw him once, when he turned the deed over to us. Later, I tried to get in touch with him—his office was in Shreveport—but . . ."

"What was your great-uncle like? I mean, did you ever form any impression of him at all?"

Patty sipped at her cooling coffee. She knit her brows in thought.

"It's really hard to remember him. I recall his short stature, his solid build, his hairy arms, his thick eyebrows. Stan, though, saw him just before he died."

Chill looked at Dr. Morgan.

"I made out the death certificate. The attorney, Mr. Duchamps, called me, and I came out. I had seen Grandier once before, when his wife, Estelle, died. She had pneumonia, and it was too late to treat her. Grandier was brusque, very untalkative. He had an accent. French, I gather."

"Of course," said Patty. "He and my great-aunt were from France. But they had lived here a long time."

"Did you find any of his papers after you took over the house?" Chill asked. "Anything they left behind?"

"No, I didn't," said Patty.

"The place was as clean as a whistle," Tom put in.

"That's odd, isn't it?" Kim asked. "I mean, usually people leave something behind. In a desk or a closet?"

"There wasn't a thing here," Patty said firmly. "Even the furniture was gone. I never did find out what happened to it. I'm sure it was all antique, too."

"I can help you there, I think," said Dr. Morgan. "There was furniture in this house, but Mr.

Duchamps said he was to ship it to another relative overseas after Mr. Grandier died. At that time, I didn't know Patty and Tom."

"Was there a will?" Chill asked.

"Yes, but it was very brief," Patty replied. "It didn't say anything about the furniture. Just that the house was ours and that the Grandiers and their family were buried here, that the tomb must not be disturbed or I would forfeit my inheritance. Silly. I never even saw the tomb. I asked Moses once where it was, and he pointed to the bluffs. I know it seems sacrilegious or something, but I wasn't terribly interested. I hate tombs, anyway. If he was worried about me disturbing it, he was wrong."

"I looked for it once," Tom said, "but couldn't find it. It's probably all grown over by now. Vegetation grows fast here. It's incredible."

"Even the garden," Patty said, then winced as if remembering her last visit there.

"Clare, let's leave these people to their family discussion," Ozzie said abruptly. "It's late and I'm tired."

"Oh, Ozzie," Clare said, "it's interesting."

"Clare—it's family talk."

"I guess you're right. Forgive me, Patty, Tom, Dr. Chillders, Dr. Morgan._We'd better get to bed. Thanks for a lovely supper. We'll be going back home tomorrow. We don't want to impose any more than we already have at a time like this."

"Oh, don't be silly, Clare," Patty said. "Stay as long as you like." But her words were flat. There was an awkward silence as the Bransons got up from the table and left, saying their "good nights."

Kim Michaels rose from her chair.

"I'm exhausted. Forgive me, Tom, Patty. It's been a long day."

"I know, Kim," Tom said sympathetically. "Thanks for helping out. See you in the morning?"

"Yes. I'll get a good night's sleep, I'm sure." She looked at Chill meaningfully.

A few moments later, Dr. Morgan got up. He realized, perhaps, that the conversation was not meant for his ears, either.

"I've got to turn in, too," he said. "I have to get up early in the morning when the nurses change shifts. It was a delightful meal. If you need more sedation, Patty, just call me."

"Good night, Stan," Patty said. "And thanks. I'm fine now." A warm bath had transformed her. There were only traces of hysteria—in her eyes and at the corners of her trembling mouth.

Tom sloshed the coffee around inside his cup. He was coming down from a sedation of his own. His mouth was furry, even after the food. He lit a cigarette, as if to keep his hands from shaking.

"You don't mind, do you, Chill?" he asked.

"They're your lungs."

Patty laughed self-consciously.

"Well," she said, "here we are. Joan's upstairs in some kind of shock, and the house is full of people who came for a party. It's kind of funny, isn't it? No, it's not funny. I don't know what I mean. I don't want to dwell on Joan, but I can't help it. I keep thinking of her up in that bed with that green mold all over her feet."

"Stop it, Patty," Tom said sharply. "That's not doing any of us any good."

"See? I have to repress everything. That's not good for me, is it?" she asked soulfully.

"Sometimes it is, sometimes not." Chill smiled warmly at her.

"You're still preoccupied, aren't you, Chill?" Tom asked, as if sensing Chill's feelings at the moment. "Is there something Patty and I ought to know, even if it's just speculation on your part?"

"I'm still thinking about the Grandiers, Tom. I want to know more about them. Patty, do you recall any vague first impressions, any little thing that you may have dismissed at the time you met them?"

"Like what, for instance?" Patty asked.

"Well, how did they treat you? You were a small girl, I gather, when you met them. Your uncle must have been quite old when he died. Do you remember if he considered you a special person, or said anything that would make you feel as though he liked you more than the rest of the family? He did, after all, deed you this place, a whole section of land, and a nice home."

"Unfurnished," Tom quipped.

The three of them laughed.

"Well, Patty?" Chill insisted.

Patty pushed her chair back from the table and crossed her legs. Tom snuffed out his cigarette in an ashtray and leaned forward, rapt.

"I—I don't know. It's hard to think. There is one thing, though." Patty ran a slender hand through her hair, than patted it back into place. "I remember the last time we visited Uncle Bernard and Aunt Estelle. I was, oh, about thirteen or so. Maybe fifteen. Uncle Bernard was about the same as he always was, grumpy, snorty, like a big dwarf with asthma, puffing on his cigar, hacking at the phlegm in his chest. We were here for a weekend, I guess. And, you know, I can remember the furniture now, Chill. It was highly polished, probably antique. Must have been Louis

XIV, at least. But that's neither here nor there. My folks went inside to talk to Estelle. I was left with Uncle Bernard, out by the . . . where the garden is now. I don't know what was there then—just a field, I think. Anyway, Uncle Bernard looked at me and sat down on a rock or a stump—I can't remember. Something. He asked me if I liked the house and visiting with them. I think I was bored stiff, but I knew how to talk to relatives, so I told him that I did."

"Get to the point, Patty," Tom said.

"I am, Tom—I'm thinking back a long way."

"Not that long," Tom grinned.

"Thank you for that, lover!"

"Go on, Patty," Chill said quietly.

"Well, he called me over to him, as I recall, and I sat on his leg—which was unusual. I mean, Uncle Bernard was always so standoffish. He wasn't a man you just warmed up to very easily. Anyway, I listened to him, since he seemed to have become almost human. He talked about the land here and a bunch of things I don't remember. What I do remember now, though, is the very strange thing he said that day."

"What was that, Patty?" Chill leaned over his cup of lemon grass tea.

"Well, he said he looked forward to my bringing my daughter to live there—after he was gone. He said he was sure she would be a beautiful girl, a proud descendant of the Grandiers."

Tom's jaw fell.

"Holy shit, Patty, you never told me that!" he said.

"I never thought of it until just now. I thought my uncle was plain crazy."

Chill took a deep breath and leaned back in his chair. He took a sip of his tea. It was cold. He set the cup back down in the saucer and looked intently at Patty.

"What do you think now?" he asked quietly.

Patty's eyes went wide, and she moved in her chair as though shaken, as though cold all of a sudden.

# CHAPTER ELEVEN

Chill listened to the purr of the phone at the other end.

He sat on the edge of his bed, munching a carob bar, waiting for Hal to pick up the phone. He looked at his watch. It was still early in Vermont, only an hour later in time. His watch showed 9:55 P.M. He crossed one leg and began untying his shoelace. In another moment, he knew, the operator would come on the line and tell him there was no answer.

He heard the operator tap into the line.

"Hello," said Harold Strong, in a tentative voice.

The operator clicked off.

"Hal, it's Chill."

"Yeah, uh, hi."

"Did I disturb you at something important?"

"Well, sort of. Indisposed and all that."

"Not one of the Bennington girls, I trust."

"No, this one's from out of state. I'm afraid you caught us at a bad moment."

"*In flagrante delicto*, no doubt."

"Close to it. What's up?"

"Hal, I don't want to spoil your evening."

"She'll keep. She has a martini to work on in my absence. Let me fill my pipe, and you can tell me the reason why you're interfering with my love life. I have some plum wine I'm chilling for a late, candle-light supper. I made it last summer, and it's ripe for the savoring."

"The wine or the woman?"

"Both."

Chill laughed and listened to the sounds of Hal tamping his pipe, then lighting it.

"Okay, I'm ready," Hal said. He was a professor of literature at Bennington College but, more importantly, he was a close friend of Chill, a dedicated chess partner, cool under pressure, and a valuable help in esoteric research. Chill used him as a sounding board whenever he was involved in his investigations of the paranormal.

"Hal, I need you out here in Louisiana. I'm near Shreveport, way out in the country. I think I've got a case of possession on my hands with some very weird kinks to it."

"Is Laura with you?"

"Not yet," Chill said tightly, removing the shoe he'd untied, uncrossing his leg and crossing the other one. He began untying the other shoe.

"What do you need?" Hal asked, after a pause.

First, I want you to check on a family named Grandier. Maybe from France. Maybe going back a long way. The name strikes a small chord in my mind, but nothing I can put together into one piece. I'm thinking of Joan of Arc, but not Joan of Arc. Further back in time. I think this involves a very ancient French family, and there may be some reference to a Grandier in the occult literature. Gregory, maybe."

"Pope Gregory the Great?"

"He dealt with possession, of course. Could be. Try them, Hal. I want a fast answer. Don't get bogged down in research."

"Giving you a bad time back there?"

"Not yet. Give me a call here as soon as you come up with something. No matter how unimportant it may seem." He gave him the phone number.

"As the boy rabbit said to the little girl rabbit, 'This won't take long, did it?' "

"Get down here, Hal," Chill said drily, stifling the urge to laugh, "as soon as you finish with the research." Hal's phone clicked dead first. Hal had raised his spirits considerably.

Chill had some research of his own to do and regretted that it meant going into Shreveport the next day. The name *Grandier* rang a small bell. If anyone could come up with an historical connection, it would be Hal Strong. In matters of research, Hal was methodical and thorough.

Hal Strong's life had been shattered a few years before when his only son, Larry, had drowned in the family pool. His wife, Patricia, had divorced him soon afterwards, leaving him alone with double grief. In a desperate search for faith, Hal had drifted into an exploration of occult matters, partly in an attempt to reach the boy beyond the grave. Because of his intensive studies, he believed his son Larry lived on in another life. His attempts to communicate with Larry led him to seek out a psychic, and that's how he met Laura Littlefawn. They became close, and then Hal introduced her to Chill.

Not long after, Laura Littlefawn became Chill's psychic sidekick and the special lady he called in for consultation on problem cases.

Hal Strong, in the meantime, continued his research for proof of life after death, reincarnation, and the existence of the soul, and he followed Chill's cases avidly, often being called upon to contribute to the solutions. Besides that, Hal also edited and proofread all of Chill's books.

Hal liked his pipe and martinis and indulged in amateur winemaking, a carryover from his days at UC Davis. He could beat Chill at chess, but not as often as he would like. If he had learned anything from Chill, it had been patience, intuition, and hope. He also enjoyed the special privilege of being excused from classes at Bennington when Chill needed him. This was a bonus he cherished, much as he enjoyed teaching literature.

Chill was damned glad that Hal was coming to Louisiana. He would have to call Laura Littlefawn first thing in the morning.

After hanging up, Chill looked over the room that Tom had assigned him. It was spacious, comfortable, modern. There was a small desk where he could keep his notebook up-to-date, a private bath, and windows overlooking the grounds at the rear of the mansion. He finished undressing as he looked out over the moonlit lawn, the garden beyond, and the thickly wooded area beyond that. He opened the window and smelled the dank air. It was like being in a greenhouse. The scent of vegetation was heavy in his nostrils.

He peered out into the contrasting layers of darkness. A few stars sprinkled the sky, which was paler than the trees that cut off the horizon. Below the treetops the darkness became impenetrable. The moon served only to heighten the effect, emphasizing dark blobs against even darker ones. The air was heavy with the scent of moss-covered cypress, their trunks thrust into the mud of a nearby lake. In the distance, he heard the haunting cry of a peacock, sounding strangely like a human call for help.

He thought of Laura Littlefawn. He would be glad to see her. It had been a long time. Too long. He hadn't seen her since his last case. Her father, John Walking Eagle, was a full-blooded Sioux from the Rosebud Reservation near Pierre, South Dakota. Her mother, Genevieve, died giving birth to her, but acted as control in all of Laura's trances. At times the rapport Laura and Chill shared was positively eerie.

Laura had an apartment in Atlanta, but Chill had never been there. It was one of Laura's many mysteries. She had never invited him there, had never mentioned its location. He had her telephone number, that was all.

Chill drew away from the window and continued undressing. He slipped into pajamas, brushed his teeth, then sat down at the desk to make notes before turning in. He was engaged in that task when he heard the faint, tentative taps at the door. He looked up from the notebook, closed it, and slid it to one side. He went to the door and opened it.

Kim slipped inside, a furtive figure in a pale blue robe.

Chill closed the door quietly. He didn't lock it.

"I can see by the blank look on your face that you weren't expecting me," she said. Her robe fell open, and he could see her breasts rising full and round as melons out of the bodice of her negligee.

"I'm sorry, Kim. I was—preoccupied."

"Oh, Chill," she laughed, "you can't help yourself, can you? When you're on a case, you're all bloodhound. Sublimating all that sexuality. *Tsk. Tsk.* Don't you think it's time you thought of yourself? And me?"

She slipped out of her robe and let it fall to the floor. She glided over to Chill and insinuated herself into his arms. He smelled her faint perfume, heady in his nostrils. Her hair was soft against his cheek. Her breasts burned into his chest.

"Kiss me," she breathed, tilting her head up, closing her eyes.

He drew her close and kissed her. Fires stirred in his loins. She pressed closer to him, her thighs insistent against his own. The kiss became more passionate. Her tongue snaked inside his mouth, a mime of what she wanted from him. Despite the suddenness of her attack, he found himself responding. Kim was, after all, a delectable woman. Delectable and sensuous. She was soft as well. He liked responsive women. While Kim had been the aggressor, perhaps because of an urgency borne of past disappointments and a yearning for Chill, it didn't take very long for Chill to assume a role more in keeping with his personality. He did enjoy being in control, and even if it was only an illusion in the present situation, it was a delightful one. Kim quickly became the subservient female, albeit a famished one, and allowed Chill to force his attentions on her. Her athletic body quickly became pliant, supple, yielding. She knew Chill was no pushover, but he could be had.

The temperature in the room rose, and it wasn't exactly attributable to the warmth of a summer eve. Chill moved his kisses from her lips to her ear, her neck, her shoulder. Kim squirmed with desire, a kittenish rapture supplanting her former boldness. Mouth open, she panted with genuine desire, adding fuel to her presence in Chill's grasping arms, pouring, in panting breath, raw alcohol onto a building flame. A strap from her gown slipped from one of her shoulders. A breast was freed from its subtle silken restraint, proving that she knew the appropriate size to purchase in the seductive nightgown line. She wriggled out from under the other strap, and with a whisper, her gown slithered to the carpeted floor. Deft fingers flew at the buttons on Chill's pajama tops. She pressed her bared breasts against his bared chest, rubbing the taut nipples against his skin and tingling hairs.

He lifted her from the floor and carried her easily over to the bed. Even if he had not exactly instigated this assignation, he was all for it now. Kim was a voluptuous marvel atop the bed, her long legs chastely held together, one knee cocked slightly, angled over her loins. A provocative portrait that Chill lustily drank in as he peeled off his unbuttoned pajama tops and slipped out of his trousers. There would be no bother about turning down the covers. The top of the spread would do just nicely for them. Chill slid into Kim's waiting arms, supplely melding his naked body to hers. Their mouths locked again, and the dance of tongues began, a less-than-subtle prelude to what they both wanted desperately.

"Oh, Chill," Kim breathed, between passionate kisses, her body a writhing mass of torrid flesh, "I've wanted this for so long. I've dreamed of it night after night. Finally, it's happening. I can't believe it!"

"I'm glad," he said, a huskiness in his voice.

She reached for his manhood then, sliding into the position she wanted.

Her hand never reached its destination.

Three things happened at once.

The phone jangled like a general-quarters alarm aboard a battleship.

The door to the room banged open with a bone-paralyzing crash.

Patty, standing in the doorway, shrieked like a startled banshee.

"Oh my God!" she exclaimed. "I'm sorry."

"Christ!" cursed Kim, her arm outstretched in midair, her hand empty, frozen in a rigid grasp. "What the hell is this?"

"Shut the damned door!" commanded Chill, sprawling out of the bed in a desperate attempt to reach the phone and strangle it into insensibility.

"I—I'm terribly sorry," mumbled Patty incoherently. "I—I thought Tom was in here. I heard—oh, dammit, both of you, I made a terrible mistake! Go ahead and screw your heads off!"

Chill scraped his knee on the rug, as he tumbled from the bed. Patty disappeared into the hall, and Kim slammed the door shut with a resounding crack, her anger turning her into an avenging angel with flashing eyes.

"Uuumph!" Chill grunted, as he struggled to his feet. The phone continued to bleat its warning. He hobbled over to it, nursing his knee, and wrenched the instrument from its cradle. "Dammit, hello!" he blared into the mouthpiece. Kim turned to stare at him, her bare breasts rising and falling, her breathing deep from her recent exertion. She had the bewildered appearance of someone suddenly forced to vacate a hotel room during a five-alarm blaze. All she saw was the backside of Dr. Russell Victor Chillders, as he seemed about to violently hump the phone sitting on the writing desk. The ludicrousness of the situation only added to her confusion.

"Laura?" Chill turned, phone to ear, so that he faced Kim. His eyes were wide with surprise. "Laura? Is this you?"

"Yes, Chill. Who did you think it was?" Her voice crackled from far away. "I hope I didn't interrupt anything too pressing." There was a measurable coating of sarcasm on her words.

"Is it . . . Laura?" Kim mouthed silently, her eyebrows raised like Roman arches.

Chill nodded at Kim.

"Where are you, Laura?" Chill asked. "I—I was going to call you."

"Tonight?" she said. "Funny, I didn't get that impression at all." There was now a decided tang to her sarcasm.

"How did you get this number?" Chill wanted to know. The phones in the house, he had learned, all had separate numbers. He hadn't known his own number until he'd called Hal, in fact.

"I talked to Tom Brunswick a while ago. He gave me the number."

"Oh. Well, I want you to come down here, Laura. Soon as you can."

"Tonight?"

The hackles rose on the back of Chill's neck. He glanced sheepishly at Kim, who remained embarrassingly naked in front of the door, her stare fixed questioningly on Chill. He wondered if Laura Littlefawn could actually *see* the room as it was now. He crossed his legs.

"Just where are you?" he asked, regaining his composure. Laura, after all, was uncanny. Her telepathic powers were a never-ending source of wonder.

"In Atlanta," Laura said cheerily. "I just got back from a grand day of tennis and a marvelous swim."

"That's good," Chill said, trying to keep the conversation on that plane. "Uh, why don't you plan on flying down to Shreveport tomorrow? I'll pick you up or have you picked up."

"Why, Chill, you mean you wouldn't want me down there tonight?"

"You're teasing me, Laura."

"Mmmmmaybeeeee," she drawled. "You're not doing anything naughty, are you? I had the strongest vibrations after I got back home. It was almost like a direct pipeline into your thoughts. I called Mrs. Ryerson, and she told me you had driven down to Tom's early. How's the party going?"

"Laura, let's stop kidding around. Joan's in trouble. She's unconscious and I've called Hal in on the case. I think we might have a case of possession."

"I already talked to Hal. But as concerned as I am for Joan, that's not why I called. No, I got the distinct impression that you were, well, it's none of my business. I just wanted you to know that I know, I guess. Catty of me, isn't it?"

Chill was speechless.

"I'll be down tomorrow. I'll let you know my flight number. Have a good time, Chill."

"Laura, wait a minute! Let me explain—"

But he heard the phone click, and knew that she had hung up. He put the receiver back in its cradle and looked wryly at Kim.

"What's going on here?" she asked. "What's Laura doing calling you at this time of night?"

Chill got up and began putting on his pajamas. He didn't look at Kim.

Kim got the message. "Broke the mood, I guess."

"It is late, Kim. I've got a lot to do tomorrow. I'm sorry the evening turned out badly."

"I don't blame you. Laura's a beautiful person. I hope you won't tell her."

Chill picked up her gown and handed it to her.

Then he walked over to Kim and put his arms around her.

"Oh, no," he said. "I wouldn't breathe a word of this to Laura." He smiled a devilish smile.

# CHAPTER TWELVE

Bernice Baines, R.N., brushed her red hair vigorously. She looked at her face in the mirror. She hardly noticed the pockmarks anymore. Or the freckles. The wrinkles had taken over and made her face into a raisin pudding. She no longer had any illusions about her looks, but she did keep her appearance neat. Her body had become chunkier over the years, and she supposed that was partly due to neglect of her sex life. Her husband had died some ten years before, and she had gone back to nursing, a job she loved but had not pursued for a number of years prior to Harry's death. She couldn't stand the daily grind of hospitals, but she enjoyed geriatric work. It made her feel young. Not that fifty-three was old, but she had been a widow for ten years, and that state of mind had taken its toll. Dr. Morgan kept her busy most of the time, but she almost wished he hadn't brought her in on this assignment.

There was something decidedly spooky about the patient, Joan Brunswick. Nurse Baines thought she ought to be in a hospital—in the Intensive Care unit. The girl's pulse was far too weak, her blood pressure way below normal, and her breathing almost nonexistent. Still, she didn't feel that it was her place to question Dr. Morgan's decision. This was a crazy house anyway. People running in and out of bedrooms at all hours of the night. Mrs. Brunswick was hysterical. She ought to be hospitalized too, Mrs. Baines thought.

Well, she'd be off the shift in a few moments. Let Francine Arnold handle the loonies all day long. All she wanted to do was to sleep and to forget that awful green mold that had been appearing in patches all over the I.V. equipment. Well, she wouldn't mention that either. Let Francine handle it if it appeared again. She had used almost a full bottle of rubbing alcohol to keep the bottle and tubing clean. The funny thing was that the girl didn't look as if she was in any danger. Her breathing, though slow, was regular. So was her pulse. There had been no change on that chart. The same with the blood pressure. And she was such a beautiful girl. A sleeping beauty. That's what she reminded her of—*Sleeping Beauty*, like the fairy tale. Well, it would take more than a handsome prince to wake this one up.

Mrs. Baines finished combing her hair. It was shining from the brushing. A shame to put it all up again, but rules were rules. Carefully, she rolled and tucked it, bobby-pinned it strategically, then put on her nurse's cap. She was hungry. Mrs. Dailey had brought her up a cup of coffee earlier, but that hadn't filled the void. She looked at her watch. She had been in the bathroom for fifteen minutes. Hurrying, she put her toiletries back in her case and zipped it shut. She put it on the floor underneath the sink. She had better give her patient one more check and enter the numbers on the chart.

Bernice Baines gasped aloud when she saw the I.V. apparatus.

The bottle of I.V. solution was completely covered

with a sticky green mold. So was the stand from which it hung. She ran around the side of the bed and looked down at the floor. From the window, there was a six-inch-wide stream of what appeared to be green slime leading to the I.V. stand. It seemed to be fed by some force that pushed it up the stand. She couldn't see it moving, but she could almost feel it.

Her training helped her overcome her fear. She reached for the plastic bottle of rubbing alcohol and the box of cotton balls. Her eyes went to the tube where the I.V. solution dripped into Joan's veins. Her hand stopped reaching. She shook her head as if to clear her eyes. The fear that she had quelled rose up in her throat. Blindly, she reached for the tubing. Her hand seemed to move in slow motion, although her brain was screaming at her to hurry. She flailed at the tubing, missing it on the first try. She lashed out again, her hand grasping the plastic tubing inches from the needle in Joan's arm. She tugged, and the needle came loose.

Seconds later, a flow of green slime mingled with the intravenous solution and oozed from the tip of the needle.

"Doctorrrrrrr Morgannnnnnn!" she yelled. The slime dripped on her shoes as she stood beside the bed, rooted there with a look of disbelief on her face.

Chill was the first to enter the room and reach Nurse Baines.

His eyes swept the scene. The nurse seemed frozen, looking blankly at the dripping needle and tube in her hand while Joan slept on peacefully. He saw the ribbon of green that flowed from the window sill, down the wall, from the baseboard, across the rug, to the I.V. stand. There was the smell of chlorophyll and swamp air in the room, the fetid aroma of rotting vegetation. He got the picture immediately.

"It's all right, Mrs. Baines," Chill said quietly. "You did well."

A moment later, Dr. Morgan and Tom came bursting into the room.

"I—I, look, Joan, she almost, oh doctor, what's going on here?"

"Easy now, Mrs. Baines. Chill?"

Chill glanced at the tube in Mrs. Baines's hand.

"The nurse here evidently stopped something terrible from happening, Dr. Morgan. That slime was just about to enter Joanie's veins."

Tom muttered an oath. He looked as though he had either slept in his clothes or hadn't slept at all.

Dr. Morgan took the tube out of the nurse's hand. He examined it closely. The green slime dripped from it at the established rate of flow for the intravenous solution.

"Tom," Chill said, "don't let anyone in here, especially Patty. Dr. Morgan, I want samples of this slimelike vegetation to send to a lab."

"Mrs. Baines, get a sterile bottle and scoop this stuff into it. Seal it. That is, if you can stand to do it without getting sick." Dr. Morgan twisted his nose in disgust.

"Yes, doctor." Baines was all efficiency, then.

"Where's Miss Arnold?" Morgan snapped.

"She's due here anytime," said the nurse.

"Chill, this is horrible!" Tom was distraught. He reeked of brandy.

"Tom, why don't you just take care of that door? Don't let anyone in except the other nurse," Chill told him. "I can't give you any answers now, and you can help by staying out of our way."

98

Tom went meekly to the door and took up his station. Nurse Baines began to spoon up the slime on the floor. She sloshed it into a urine specimen bottle and corked it. Chill put it in his pocket. A few moments later, Francine Arnold knocked on the door. Tom let her in. The rest of the household, apparently, hadn't stirred yet.

"Could you help her clean up before you go off, Mrs. Baines?" Dr. Morgan asked. "As you can see, Miss Arnold, there's quite a mess here."

"What is it?" asked the younger nurse. "It's slimier than that other green mold."

"Just a leak in the roof or something, I imagine," said Morgan. "It's messy, and I hate to ask you to be chorewomen, but this is an unusual situation. I want to check the patient while you both help out here."

"Mrs. Dailey can give you a mop and buckets," Tom said. "I'm sure she's puttering around in the kitchen."

"Fine. You women go on downstairs and get what you need. I'll take over here." Morgan picked up Joan's chart and began reading the figures. He let the intravenous tube fall to the floor.

"I've got to get some coffee, Stan," Tom piped in from his position at the door. His face was pasty, and his eyes had a look of pleading in them.

"If you think my eyes look bad, you should see them from the inside." Tom was gone before either man could reply. Chill and Morgan looked at each other and shrugged.

"The chart shows that she's been stable all night," Morgan said.

"I just wonder if we need the I.V. anymore. Might be dangerous with this slime so aggressive."

"What the hell do you make of that?"

99

"I liked your explanation about the leak in the roof, Dr. Morgan, but just between us, I'd say we had a sentient process here. There is an intelligence at work." Chill said.

"Do you mean someone is causing this to happen?"

"Not necessarily. Not 'someone' living, anyway. I mean that there could be an intelligent vegetable process at work here."

"Oh, come on, Chill, you can't be serious. I've heard about *The Secret Life of Plants* and all that. Screaming tomatoes. Nervous philodendrons."

"Biologists can't even define 'life' in all its forms, doctor. But I'd say that everything that exists is 'alive.' That is it is composed of living molecules, energy, matter that continues to function in one form or another as long as the universe holds together. This isn't exactly original thinking on my part, of course. The Indian tribes believed the very same thing. And before you get on my case about jabbering tomatoes and hypertensive house plants, let me lay some groundwork on you. The medicine you use today is made from living organisms. The pharmaceutical companies had to go back to the Indians for the recipes. Every time they get stuck on a problem, they send a scientist out to the boonies to check on the shamans and the old witch doctors to find out how they mixed up certain herbs, bits of earth, ground-up stone, clay, flowers, parts of animals and insects, fish bone, and bird wings into medicinal products according to formulas dating back thousands of years."

"I'm aware of all that, Chill. There's still a lot of hocus-pocus connected with the use of those primitive remedies."

"All right. Acupuncture works, too. So does the 'laying on of hands.' Anything works if you believe in it.

I believe that the plant kingdom does have a certain intelligence. We may not be able to translate all of its language yet, but we will, someday. We may be able to communicate with plants, as well as dolphins and other creatures, if we try hard enough. What I'm saying here is that this flowing slime and the mold that appeared on Joan's feet and bed yesterday were *intelligently controlled*. It didn't just appear because of humidity or atmospheric conditions. You'll notice that the slime moves from that window in a direct, unwavering path, toward Joan's bed and the I.V. stand. Somehow it infiltrated itself into that bottle of liquid nourishment and was headed down the tube with the intention of getting into that girl's veins." Chill took the bottle from the stand and examined it. "Here look at this, doctor."

Dr. Morgan looked at the portion of tubing in Chill's hands. Chill rubbed the slime away from the part that was coming out of the neck of the bottle.

"See? A small pinhole. Eaten away. Looks like acid." Chill held the bottle upside down, the way it hung on the stand. "And, notice. The slime first pushed upward, mingling with the solution. *Upward!*"

"Damn!" Morgan exclaimed. "I never noticed that before. I think you're right."

"So how did that happen? How did the slime run *up* the stand? Why did it do that? Why does it want to get inside Joan's veins?"

"I don't know!" Morgan shouted, obviously upset. "None of this makes any sense! It's uncanny."

"It sure is. I'm going to have this slime examined by a friend of mine, a scientist with the Center for Disease Control in Atlanta—Rudy Kellerman. I want to find out the properties of this junk—whether it's toxic, what it would do in the human system—if I can, if Rudy can tell me. In the meantime, I suggest we both keep open minds about the events that occur here. We won't get anywhere if we're at each other's throats all the time."

"You seem to forget that I'm the physician in charge here, Chill. I still don't buy this plant intelligence theory."

"But you must admit that something extraordinary has occurred here."

"I can't treat my patient with extraordinary procedures, however. I must use the technology that's available."

"Even at the risk of her life? Look, doctor, I'm going to override you on this. I want Joan off the I.V.—now! You can continue to monitor her vital signs if you wish. I'm going to try to check out the source of this green fluid that's getting in here. You'll notice it's stopped flowing for the moment."

Morgan glanced down at the rug. The slime was being absorbed into the fabric and was no longer moving toward Joan's bed.

"I'll get this sample off to Kellerman today when I go into town. I'll see if I can find something to kill the organisms in this slime to keep it from spreading so fast. If I can, perhaps we can prevent any further encroachment of mold or slime on Joan's bed."

"If we moved her to the hospital—"

"We wouldn't find out a damned thing."

"Look, Chill, I think I've shown plenty of patience with you. Joan is still my patient until either Tom or Patty tells me different. I'll thank you not to interfere anymore."

Morgan began to check the instruments at Joan's bedside. He took her pulse. With his stethoscope, he listened to her heartbeat. Chill went to the window and looked out. He opened it, leaned over the side of the house, and looked down. Ivy covered the wall of the house; it was thick, clinging. The sun was just coming up and moving the shadows across the expanse of lawn at the side of the house. The slime seemed to have oozed from a source he could not determine from his vantage point. It disappeared into the tangle of vines a short distance down from the window. He would have to go downstairs to check its origin.

He wished he wasn't having trouble with Morgan. He needed him, despite his stubborness. He knew he was out of line in ordering the doctor to stop the I.V., but it was a decision he felt necessary. He didn't dare risk Joan's life by giving the slime a chance to enter her body.

The nurses returned to the room with mops, pails, ammonia and soap. They began to scrub the rug. Disgust showed on their faces as they wrung the slimy substance into the pails. They shot dirty looks in Chill's direction, as if he were to blame. Or, he thought, maybe it was because he had challenged the doctor, their superior. Even as they worked, Chill noticed, the green substance was already disintegrating, drying up, turning into a dusty mold. Or was it, he wondered, impregnating itself into the wood underneath the rug, leaving only these signs of its passing?

"Thank you, Mrs. Baines," Dr. Morgan said. "You'd better get some sleep. Thanks. You did a good job here."

"Thank you, Dr. Morgan." She glanced at Chill. "I am rather tired. See you tonight, Francine."

"Sleep well," said Francine.

"Miss Arnold," Morgan said tightly, "I want a blood sample from the patient. Get at least 40 cc."

"Right away, doctor."

Morgan made some notations on the chart.

Chill waited to see if Morgan would order the I.V. started again.

"Hold up on the I.V. for the time being, Miss Arnold, but let me know immediately if there is any change in the patient's condition. Keep an eye on the monitors at all times."

"Yes, doctor."

"There's been no urine in twenty-four hours," Morgan said to Chill. "No elimination from either the bowels or the bladder. I think it might be dangerous to halt the I.V. at this time."

"Let's go downstairs, Morgan. We can talk there." Chill felt he would get nowhere arguing with Morgan in front of his nurse. Besides, it was two against one. He was sure that Miss Arnold felt the same as Mrs. Baines—hostile toward him.

Morgan gave his patient a last look. Joan's color was good. She looked healthy, peaceful. He leaned over, pulled back an eyelid. He was rewarded with a vacant, staring eye. There was no movement. He took a pencil flashlight from his pocket and flashed it in Joan's eye. The pupil did not change size. He let the eyelid fall back into place and rammed his penlight back into his pocket. He took a deep breath, pulled his stethoscope from around his neck, and stuffed it into his hip pocket.

"I'll see you in a while, Miss Arnold."

"Don't worry, doctor. I'll call you if there's any change. Are there to be any visitors?"

Chill shook his head.

"Not unless I tell you otherwise," Morgan said.

"Yes, *doctor*." Her emphasis didn't escape Chill's notice.

Chill and Morgan went downstairs. They didn't speak on the way. They found the breakfast nook, where Mrs. Dailey had been serving coffee. Chill went into the kitchen while Morgan sat down at the table.

"Dr. Morgan would like some coffee, Mrs. Dailey," he told the maid. "I just need some hot water. I brought my own tea."

"Good morning, Dr. Chillders. I know. Mrs. Brunswick told me several days ago about what kind of foods you eat. I'll bring the coffee and some hot water for you. Want any breakfast? I mean does the other doctor?"

"I don't know. I doubt it. You can ask him when you bring the coffee."

"How's Joan—Miss Brunswick? I heard noises upstairs a while ago."

"She's fine. Sleeping soundly."

"If you ask me, one of you had better doctor Mr. Brunswick. He doesn't look at all well this morning."

"No, I imagine not. Have you seen Mrs. Brunswick this morning? Or any of the guests?"

"Nope. All sound asleep. Humph! If you ask me, the whole lot of them ought to shinny on home."

"Yes. Well, I'm sure Mrs. Brunswick will handle things when she gets up."

Chill sat down across the table from Morgan.

"Coffee'll be here in a minute." Chill drew a packet from an envelope in his pocket. "I'm having tea."

"Your own brand?" There were no markings on the square-cut tea bag. There was also no string.

"Red Zinger. Rosehips, hibiscus flowers, lemon grass, peppermint, some orange peel, wild cherry bark, and a dash of wintergreen. Place in Boulder,

105

Colorado, puts it out—Celestial Seasonings. Lots of Vitamin C in it."

"Never heard of it," Morgan snorted.

"Doctor, let's get down to cases. I don't want to get in your hair. You don't want to get in mine. We've got a girl upstairs we're both concerned about. She's out of it. Reasons unknown at present. We've got a distraught father who's got some personal problems. The mother is also on edge. If we don't work together and get things under control, I think we're going to have a houseful of disturbed people. We've got enough problems trying to figure out how to help Joan. Agreed?"

"Agreed. But there is only one physician on this case. I hardly think I have to remind you."

Chill could see that he was getting nowhere.

Mrs. Dailey brought the coffee and the cups. She poured hot water in Chill's cup. He tossed the tea bag in it. Soon the water turned blood red. Both men stared at the darkening stain in the cup for a long time, without speaking.

"Joan is still my patient. I won't have my authority undermined," Morgan said coldly and finally.

*You bastard*, Chill thought.

He sipped his red tea, staring at Morgan. His eyes were dark, cold.

# CHAPTER THIRTEEN

Patty woke with a queasiness in her stomach.

She felt an almost overwhelming sense of vertigo when she sat up on the edge of the bed. She closed her eyes to shut out the spinning room.

She knew the feeling. It was like the other times, outside in the garden.

She clenched her teeth, fought down the nausea, the sickening taste of bile rising up in her throat. It took her several moments to overcome the urge to throw up. She put out her hands to steady herself, and opened her eyes. She looked at the bed. Tom had finally come to bed, but he was not there now. His side of the bed was damp from his sweat. She could still smell the reek of brandy on his breath. Damn him!

Tom had made a fool of himself chasing after Ginger. The little tramp. She had made a fool of herself, too, breaking into Chill's room like that. How could she face him? Her stomach churned again. She blinked back tears and took a deep breath to clear her mind.

Tom and Ginger had been on the back patio, both of them drinking and necking like teenagers. It was disgusting. Yet she could hardly blame Tom. He was a desperate man, she knew. She had seen the signs for a long time—seen this coming—but she hadn't admitted it to herself. Oh, she didn't think his frustration about work would focus on some teenager the likes of Ginger, but circumstances had taken care of that. Ginger had been the catalyst to push her husband over the edge. The Bransons didn't seem to give a damn, either. Ginger was slightly star struck, coming on to Tom like that. He represented a life she probably yearned for—the glamour of television, Hollywood, all that was exciting to a young girl. And Tom had fallen for her adoration. Well, he was ripe for Ginger. She had been in the right place at the right time. Tom had not been himself since Joan's collapse, either. He was particularly vulnerable.

She was bound and determined that this was not going to end in tragedy. It may have been wrong to drag Tom off to bed like that last night, but it was better than having him arrested for statutory rape or having to pay for an abortion. She had trusted Tom all these years, but he was out of his element now. This wasn't his milieu. She knew that now. At first, she had believed that Tom would come to love this place—the privacy, the seclusion, the solitude. He had said as much. But he was unable to adjust. The madcap world of television production was in his veins. He missed the excitement—the daily, hourly decisions, the scramble for ratings, the Big Apple, Beverly Hills, Malibu. Yes, she now was sure that this place was wrong for Tom. And now Joan was . . . was . . . what? Sick? Crazy? Catatonic? And what about herself? These spells?

Patty pushed herself off the bed. Her feet touched the floor. It felt good to feel something solid underneath her. She stood up, trembling slightly, like an invalid rising after long confinement. She began to walk toward the bathroom, stepping like a tightrope walker. She seemed frail in her loose pajamas. She could tell there were dark, puffy circles under her eyes. She was weary, wearier than she had ever been before. Somehow she must help Tom get a grip on himself. Somehow she must help herself, as well. She felt the need to confide in someone—someone she could trust. Chill! Chill would know what to do. He always did. Besides, she owed him a quiet, sober apology for last night. How was she to know that he and Kim? . . .

She was halfway to the bathroom when her feet seemed to sink underneath her. It felt as if she was walking on rubber. One minute she was on solid carpeted flooring, the next, she was sinking straight down. The room tilted and blurred as she tried to bring it into focus. Walking was an effort. It was like being on a loose trampoline. The floor sagged beneath her, then rose up again to tip her off-balance. The walls tilted inward, then billowed outward as though manipulated by an unseen bellows. Her vision was distorted. The bathroom door twisted and writhed as she carefully made her way toward it, barefooted. She hadn't had the energy to put on her slippers. It was important to get to the bathroom, where she could be sick if she wanted to, where she could look at herself in the mirror, establish some contact with reality. She felt the way she had in the garden—almost disembodied, something inside her wrenched out of place.

Gradually, she inched forward, arms outstretched to help her maintain her balance, then flailing wildly in the air as she succumbed to the slow gyrations of the topsy-turvy room. The queasy feeling in her stomach was subsiding somewhat, although a sudden lurch

109

would bring it back if she didn't concentrate. She made her way to the bathroom like a drunken sailor trying to walk an imaginary line.

The bathroom door was ajar. She reached the doorway, grasped the sides for support, and steadied herself against the sickening, swaying floor beneath her feet. She looked down a blurred corridor to the mirror. Her face came into misty focus, pale and drawn, but *her* face, at least. She closed her eyes for a moment and breathed a sigh of relief. The pills were in the medicine cabinet. She would be all right if she could get one of the pills down her throat, into her stomach. It was not far to the cabinet, the sink.

Patty lurched forward. Her momentum carried her to the sink. She fumbled to open the cabinet and found the envelope with the pills inside. She shook one into her hand. She pulled a Solo cup from the wall dispenser and filled it with water. She swallowed the pill: it stuck in her throat. She washed it down with a gulp of water. The cup dropped out of her hand, into the sink. She put the packet of pills back into the cabinet and held onto the sink for support. She managed a wan smile at the mirror. She would be all right now.

The queasiness subsided. She began to breathe normally again. The floor settled down and became solid under her feet. The mirror lost its wavy effect. No longer did she feel as if she were on the pitching deck of a ship. Sanity returned along with the calm; fear receded as the somatic situation improved.

So it was physical, after all. A kind of seasickness that could be cured with a simple little pill.

Patty looked at her image in the mirror and again managed a weak grin. A grinning pixie peered back at her.

Something wet spattered the top of her nose. She could see the spot it made in the mirror.

Her grin froze into a grimace of horror.

She looked up at the ceiling.

It was covered with a dripping ooze, and the slime began splattering her in gobs, covering her face, her hair, her flimsy pajamas, her arms, her hands.

She screamed for the second time in two days.

Her scream carried throughout the house. It was a steady, terror-stricken sound that had only one tone.

She was still screaming when Chill—the first on the scene, followed by Dr. Morgan—burst into the bathroom. He nearly slipped to his knees on the slime that covered the floor tiles. He wrenched Patty away from the sink, dragging her back into the bedroom. He closed her mouth and slapped her silent.

Morgan helped him carry her to the bed.

Tom came in a moment later, followed by Mrs. Dailey. There was a scramble of voices and confusion.

"Get something to clean her off," Chill told Mrs. Dailey. "Hurry."

"Patty, my God!" Tom exclaimed.

"I'd better give her sedation," said Dr. Morgan, who rushed out of the room to get his bag from Joan's bedroom.

Chill took his handkerchief from his pocket and wiped Patty's face, cleaning off the mass of green slime. She stared up at him gratefully, while Tom looked on in anguish.

"Patty," her husband said, "I—I'm so sorry. I—I don't know how to make things up to you."

She reached out her hand.

"We have to talk, Tom—but not now."

Chill crumpled up the handkerchief. He turned to Tom.

111

"Go ahead, you two. I'll catch you both later. I have a lot to do this morning. Dr. Morgan will take care of you, Patty. Don't worry about Joan. She's going to be just fine."

Patty needed Tom's strength now. Chill was sure that Tom would give it to her, and he didn't think Ginger Branson would be a problem anymore. She was, Chill thought, only a manifestation of Tom's other difficulties. He would get to those later.

Right now, it was important to get the sample of vegetation off to Atlanta. He could mail it in Shreveport and pick up Hal Strong at the same time. Before he left, however, he wanted to check the grounds below Joan's window. There was something he had to find out, if only to support a growing theory he had about the circumstances of her strange sleeping state.

Chill was elated.

Hal and Laura had phoned. They had decided to meet in Atlanta and fly to Shreveport together. That would solve some of his problems. He needed them both desperately.

His search of the grounds had reinforced his theory that supernatural forces were at work on the Grandier place. He had looked specifically for a hose or some sign of a pump. He wanted to check further, but he was convinced that the green slime had not been pumped from some spot around the house. He had found no stagnant water within a convenient distance, either. He had tried to scale the wall by pulling himself up on the vines, but they were not strong enough to support his weight. And the roof's pitch precluded anyone getting on top of the house and pouring slime down a hose through the window into Joan's room. There were traces of slime at ground level on the wall below her window. So the stuff had oozed upward from the flower beds. He had found no footprints, either. It was puzzling, but he was counting on Laura Littlefawn and her psychic ability to provide an explanation. Or on his own luck.

He drove away from the Grandier place along the country road, seeing it from a different point of view than he had the day before, when he had driven in. The Grandier place was definitely remote, surrounded by deep woods. He saw no other signs of habitation until he drove onto North Lake Shore Drive and turned toward Shreveport.

Cross Lake was huge, and the shore was dotted with only a few private homes, most of them rundown but obviously once expensive and attractive. On the opposite side of the road, black settlements—tenements in the woods, really—were bustling with life. There seemed to be a sheriff's patrol car every few hundred yards, each one surrounded by a mob of poorly dressed black people all talking and gesticulating at once.

He stopped at a gas station in Shreveport to fill the station wagon's tank, and had the oil, battery, and water checked. He then drove to Dr. Morgan's office on Cyprus Street and dropped off Joan's blood samples, with instructions to Morgan's nurse, Dolores Stevens, that they were to be analyzed in the lab right away and the report phoned out to the house as soon as it was ready.

"I know you," Miss Stevens said to Chill. An attractive raven-haired woman in her early thirties, she handled the outer office for Morgan and his partners in Lake Clinic. "I know where it was! The Phil Donohue Show! Last month! You're the psychic guy. Chillson."

113

"Chillders," he laughed. "I was on Phil's show a while back."

"What's going on out there at the Brunswicks'?"

"I'm just a guest. I was coming into town, and Dr. Morgan asked me to drop these samples off."

"I'll get them to our lab right away. Are you sure you're not looking for a ghost out there? I mean, well, it was a pretty interesting program."

"Tom Brunswick's an old friend of mine. His daughter's sick, that's all. I'm not looking for any ghosts."

"Well, I'm relieved to hear that," Miss Stevens laughed. "I'm sure happy to have met you, Dr. Chillders."

"Maybe I'll see you again," he said, waving goodbye. He could feel the nurse's eyes on his back as he went out the door.

Next, Chill went to the Hall of Records, where he poured over plat books and records for a half an hour, making notations on his yellow pad. He asked for the file on death certificates from the previous years. Gradually, his store of information was accumulating. There were numerous question marks floating about in his mind, but the biggest unknown factor was Joan herself. Somehow he had to find out why she was singled out as a victim, for that's how he was coming to view her—as an unwitting victim in the most puzzling case he had ever encountered.

He made another stop, at the Shreveport Public Library. In the science section he found what he wanted. He made more notes. He asked the clerk where he might find a health food store. The girl, young, willowy, and wearing no make-up, seemed pleased at his question. Gladly, she gave him directions. She told him that they served lunch there.

"Good." said Chill. "I was hoping they would. I'm starved."

"Well, maybe I'll see you there, if I can get off. My relief hasn't shown up yet."

"I'll buy you lunch if you make it," Chill promised.

"Hey, far out. My name's Sally!"

"They call me Chill," he said, grinning at her as he walked away.

He didn't see her snap her fingers together as recognition dawned on her. A moment later she was riffling through the *Index to Authors* to confirm her observation.

The health food store was on Magnolia, a private home converted to a combination restaurant and natural foods outlet. It sat back off the street some 25 yards. The frame house was at least eighty years old, and it was freshly painted a muted red, with white trim. The modest but artistic sign, a steal from Peter Max, proclaimed it The Bough-ery, the "original" natural foods store. There were large trees surrounding the house-store, in fact, but Chill had seen literally dozens of "original" health food stores in his travels. He gathered that each was "original" only in its own particular region.

He had a glass of carrot juice, a salad made with organically grown tomatoes, lettuce, radishes, mushrooms, celery, raw cashew nuts, and avocados. He sprinkled this with bran flakes and poured Hanes bleu cheese dressing over it. There was no sign of Sally, the girl in the library, which was just as well. Time was slipping by, and he still had more to do before the plane from Atlanta got in. He bought carob bars, sesame sticks, and assorted fresh vegetables to take back to the Brunswick place. The bearded pro-

115

prietor, a healthy looking blonde giant whose name was Todd, loaded a box for him. Todd's wife, Michele, thanked Chill and asked him to come back. As he drove away, he saw Sally ride up on a bicycle. She didn't see him. It was just as well. He would have felt compelled to return and have a second lunch.

Shreveport Regional Airport was 5 miles southwest of the city. Chill drove there at a leisurely pace, reflecting on the small accomplishments of the day. Hal and Laura would be great assets to him now. Still, there were areas of investigation that would require his personal attention. And there wasn't much time. He had a hunch that Joan's "illness" had been preordained—a long time ago. Its timing was crucial. It would be hard to check, and he couldn't wait for proof. He had to move on the assumption he was right. If not, her life was forfeit. He believed in coincidences, yes, but in this case he felt that there was no coincidence: Joan Brunswick would be sixteen years old in two days. Somehow, he believed that her birthdate was a deadline, a deadly deadline. He meant to see that she lived to celebrate her birthday!

Chill parked his wagon in a loading zone. He dashed in to the air freight desk and handed over his package containing the sample from Joan's room. Kim had wrapped it well and according to regulations: she'd had experience shipping film and videotape for Brunswick Productions. Rudy Kellerman would have the package inside of two hours. His instructions were to call Chill as soon as he learned something. Chill had talked to him earlier that morning, stressing the importance of the lab test. Rudy would come through for him. He always had.

Hal Strong waved to Chill as he came through the boarding gate, pipe clenched in his teeth, attaché case firmly in the grip of his other hand. A moment later, Chill spotted Laura a few feet behind Hal. There was no mistaking her tall figure, and her raven hair, gleaming blue-black in the sun. Moments later, Chill was pumping Hal's hand and patting the short-cropped hair on the top of his head. Then Laura was in his arms, her jade and silver bracelets pressing into his back as she squeezed him. There was a magnetism between them that went unspoken.

"I'm glad to see you two!" Chill exclaimed. "I'm glad you both came together. There isn't much time. Let's get your luggage. I'm parked right outside the terminal."

"Chill," Laura said, her husky voice carrying a sense of urgency, "you're right about that. I feel we've got to get out to Tom's place as soon as possible."

"That's right, Chill," Hal said. "She started getting impressions just as we were landing. The only impression I got was the smell of oil and cotton."

"What impressions?" Chill asked, his scalp prickly.

"I'm not sure," said Laura, as they walked across the terminal toward the baggage check-out area. "Someone's in grave danger out there. I don't know if it's a man or a woman. Hal may be smelling oil and cotton, but I smell something else."

"What's that?" Chill asked, almost afraid of her answer.

"Decay. Decaying vegetation. Like a swamp or a stagnant pond."

Chill's eyes went dark.

# CHAPTER FOURTEEN

Ozzie paced the room like a caged panther, anger in every step, every movement.

Ginger was in tears, her shoulders shivering from the effort to control her sobs.

Father and daughter were alone in the room. Clare Branson was downstairs, starting her own private cocktail hour two hours early.

"You're going to screw up everything!" Ozzie growled at his daughter. "I'm trying to get on as Tom's attorney. I want to have him as a client and as a friend. Oh, I saw you coming on to him yesterday. I thought you'd have sense enough to keep your damned hot pants to yourself."

"It wasn't me, Daddy. Not entirely. Tom likes me. He—he told me so!"

"Christ! You caught Tom off-guard. He was half drunk, and upset about his daughter. He's going through some kind of personal crisis in his business, in his life. His wife's a nervous wreck, and here you come along, shaking your ass at him and baring your tits! What the hell do you expect?"

"Stop it! Stop talking that way!"

Ozzie glared at his daughter. She had been swimming and was still wearing her bathing suit. She sat on a towel she had put on a chair. Her strawberry hair was wet and clung to her head. He looked at her damp breasts bulging out of the bra, her nipples showing through the fabric. She had her mother's hautiness, his own doughy features. She was a woman in a girl's body. She was Clare twenty-five years ago, and he didn't like to think of that. Clare had been a tramp, a martini-hog even then, but she had managed to keep it under control all these years, until lately. Now she was letting go of herself and turning into a lush. It couldn't happen at a worse time. Their daughter was pulling away from them, and when he most needed Clare, she was no use to him at all. His world was crumbling, and they both were acting like a couple of sluts.

"Don't sass me, Ginger!" He stopped pacing, but kept his distance. He didn't trust himself close to his daughter while his anger was so heated. He could feel the violence building in him. "You've been coming on to my law partners the same way. You don't date boys your own age. It's disgusting!"

"No, no," she sobbed, knowing what he said was true.

"Did you see the Brunswicks at lunch? They hardly spoke to each other. Because of you! When I saw you last night, you looked like a whore! Your lipstick was smeared, your blouse wrinkled, you—you looked like a pig!"

Ginger stood up quickly, clenching her fists.

"Why can't I do what I want to? I'm not bothering you. I didn't beg Tom to kiss me! He wanted me. So do your filthy old partners!"

"Shut up, you goddamned brat! Tom can't help himself! You're a goddamned little prick teaser. You invite these attentions from older men. You parade

119

around in front of them, wearing those sexy clothes, your tits falling out. You don't even wear a bra!"

"No, I don't wear a bra! I don't have to! I'm not doing anything wrong! I like older men! Can't you just leave me alone!"

"Quit your yelling!" He stepped over to her, his face livid with fury. "I won't leave you alone! You're not going to ruin Tom's life or anyone else's! I—I'll send you away—to a school! They'll straighten you out!"

"No you won't, Daddy! I won't go anywhere! I hate you! I hate you!"

He raised his hand, hardly knowing what he was doing. He lashed out at her with the flat of his palm, striking her hard on her cheek. She was knocked backward. The chair fell over. She screamed and struggled to her feet.

"Don't hit me!" she screamed. "Don't you ever hit me again! Do you know why I come on to Tom and the others? Don't you know?"

Ozzie's stomach turned, and he became sick inside. He gasped for breath. There was a constriction in his chest.

"No!" he shouted back.

She edged away from him, cringing, his finger marks streaking her face.

"Because of you!" she said. "You never pay any attention to me! I don't want them! I want you, Daddy, but you can't see it! You'd rather have my drunken mother. That's what's disgusting. You and she! She's a slob, and you put up with it!"

She broke down, then, the sobs racking her body. She turned back into a child, a helpless child.

"Will you shut your filthy mouth?!"

Ozzie couldn't help himself. He stormed at her, his

fists lashing out. He tried to stop, but he couldn't. He couldn't face what she was saying to him. His own daughter! He struck her again and again. He was yelling something, but he didn't know what it was. He was yelling his hatred of her, his hatred of her truth. He had tried to ignore it for a long time. He saw her through a red film of self-loathing, a haze of self-hatred.

"It's not true," he said. "It's not true." He stopped hitting her. Her lip was swollen, bleeding. One eye was puffed up. There were red welts on her shoulders and arms.

She looked at him, her eyes slitted, cold.

"Ginger, I . . . I . . ." He couldn't finish. He hung his head, trying to breathe. He was going to be sick. He hurried into the bathroom, trying to shut the terrible sight of her out of his eyes, his brain. Her accusing eyes haunted him, following him into the bathroom. He leaned over the toilet bowl. The retching began, ripping his throat and lungs, turning his stomach over. He gagged and strangled, choking on the digested food boiling up from his belly. Tears welled up in his eyes.

"I'm so sorry, Ginger. I'm so sorry," he wept, knowing she couldn't hear him. The tears that came were for her now.

He washed his face and gargled with a mouthwash. The stale taste of sickness was still in his mouth. His stomach felt raw, torn.

He went into the bedroom, hoping he could apologize to his daughter. He was ashamed of himself. He was ashamed for having seen her attentions and never facing their implications before. As Clare's periods of drunkenness had become more frequent, Ginger had had to take on more and more responsibility in running the home. The excuses for Clare's absence at social events had become more and more difficult to concoct. Gradually, without any of them realizing its implications, Ginger had usurped her mother's role in the home. She had done much of the cooking, often serving Ozzie dinner, dining with him while Clare lay passed out in the living room or in the bedroom.

Clare wasn't a bar hopper. Not any more. She had managed to conceal her alcoholism for twenty-five years, but the last three or four had been a nightmare for Ozzie and Ginger. Because of Ozzie's position in the community, they had not sought professional help. Ozzie kept hoping Clare would come to her senses. He knew that she had an incurable disease that infected all of them. Ginger had tried to take her mother's place as a homemaker and resented the fact that she couldn't share her mother's bed and husband as well. It was all too clear now.

Ozzie knew he had to get help. He knew he had to apologize to Ginger. Could she ever forgive him for what he had done? Could she ever realize how he had tried to ignore the signals she was giving him, signals that had been too painful to accept?

He stopped short when he saw the bathing suit. The two pieces lay in a puddle on the floor.

Ginger was gone!

With a cold knife of sorrow in his heart, Ozzie realized that he wouldn't be able to explain anything to her right now. He reached into his pocket. The car keys were still there. Maybe she was just sulking somewhere. He'd look around for her, ask if anyone had seen her. He didn't want anyone else to know what had happened. But he was afraid. There was something wrong about this house and the people in it. There were too many intangibles; he didn't want his daughter to become one of them. He hurried from the room, trying to quell his rising fear. He had to find her. He had to explain that he understood her now. He had to tell her that he was sorry.

Chill turned off North Lake Shore Drive onto the dirt road that led to the Brunswicks' house. He had driven too fast from town and gotten a ticket from a lake patrolman for speeding. The delay had rankled him because from what Laura had said, he knew they had no time to waste. Before being stopped, he had explained to Hal and Laura everything that had happened to date, skipping his hunches and what he had dug up in Shreveport. For the time being, he wanted them to know only the facts as they existed. That was enough input for them. Let them work independently until they all had another talk. He wanted to see what each came up with. That was Chill's method. It had worked in the past. He hoped it would work now.

"How much farther?" asked Hal. "All I see is jungle."

"Couple of miles now."

"Hal's been traveling longer than I have. All the way from Vermont. We had lunch on the plane, but no cocktails. He's probably ready for a few after what you told us about Tom and Mrs. Branson."

"Unfair, Laura, unfair. Besides, I have the idea we'll be too busy for socializing. Right, Chill?"

"It looks that way. If my hunch is right, the operative demon at work here is using Joan's birthday as the deadline. That's Sunday. This is Friday. Not much time to do all that has to be done. I may have to get a

123

court order to open the Grandier tomb. First, though, I want to have a look at it. Moses knows more than he's telling. And if that weren't enough, Tom has personal problems that need straightening out. Clare Branson appears to be an alcoholic. Ozzie Branson seems to be a decent sort, but holding back some inner conflict concerning Clare and his daughter, Ginger. I sense a rivalry between those two. The dynamics of that relationship seem to be worked out inappropriately: Ozzie clams up; Clare gets stoned; Ginger goes after older men."

"The eternal triangle," Hal said wryly. "Human relationships can get very sloppy."

"Surely, you're not suggesting that Ozzie's daughter is . . ." Laura's voice trailed off.

"Displacing her affections? Perhaps," said Chill. "Hal, I hope you've got what I'm looking for. I want to talk to you about it at the house."

"I did. The name fits, anyway."

"Grandier?"

"Grandier." Hal lit his pipe. The aroma of Mixture 79 floated in the smoke, which was sucked away from the pipe by the air conditioning.

"You think there's a demon at work here?" Laura asked Chill. She was sitting in the front seat, between the two men. She wore a peasant blouse with a pleated skirt. Her slender legs angled toward Hal's.

"I think so. The force seems to be an ancient one—using plant life. Very primitive but very powerful."

"Earth," said Laura. "The house shook, you said."

"So it would seem. The tomb could tell us something, I think." Chill reached into his pocket, pulled out a sesame stick, and popped it into his mouth—a sign that he was absorbed in his thoughts. Hal and Laura were silent as he chewed quietly on the stick.

Chill turned off the dirt road.

"This is it," he said. Shortly, the house came into view, a white glare in the afternoon sun. It was framed by continuous greenery, stark against the clear blue skyline.

"Nice place," said Hal.

"Surely you're joking," said Laura.

"At least the door doesn't creak," Hal commented, as they entered the front door of the Grandier mansion.

"We'll find Tom and Patty—get you settled," Chill said, setting down Laura's suitcase. "Leave your bag here, Hal." Hal set his suitcase down and kept his attaché case. Everything seemed serene.

Tom saw them from the top of the stairs. He waved and came down.

"Laura—good to see you again," he said, giving her a hug.

"Tom, this is my friend, Hal Strong. Hal, shake hands with Tom Brunswick."

"I've heard a lot about you, Tom. You did a hell of a job on that special with Chill and Laura."

"Thanks. Chill, Ginger's missing. No cause for alarm, probably. Her father's frantic, though. Of course, Clare's using her disappearance as an excuse to get drunk. Patty's upstairs resting. Ozzie and Moses are out back waiting for us. Ozzie's afraid she might be wandering around in the woods or in the swamp."

Laura shot Chill a look. Chill's eyes narrowed.

"How's Joan?" he asked.

"The same. Stan did another EKG on her, said she

125

was stable. He and the nurse are with her. The other nurse is asleep."

"Good. Let's get going, then. Hal, do you want to come with us?"

"Sure."

"Mrs. Dailey can show you your room, Laura. I'll tell her to meet you here on my way out. Come on, Chill, Hal. Let's get out there. This is all I need—Ginger wandering around out there, getting hurt or something."

"Here, Laura, hang on to this for me," Hal said, handing her his attaché case. They left Laura standing there and went out through the kitchen.

Tom's face was drawn. His hands trembled slightly. Chill looked at him with concern as they walked across the wide expanse of lawn toward the three figures standing at the fringe of the woods.

"Like to talk to you later, Tom," Chill said.

"Yeah. We have to talk. I've got a lot to get off my chest."

"How's Patty?"

"Better. We talked. It was a long time coming. I've been a fool."

Chill patted his friend on the back.

"Don't worry, Tom. Remember what you used to say all the time?"

"Yeah. Everything's going to be all right."

"Just keep thinking that way."

Kim was waiting with Moses and Ozzie Branson. She wore jeans and a T-shirt that clung to her body, emphasizing her breasts. She was wearing a bra. Her hair was tied back. She looked youthful except for the dark worry circles around her eyes. She smiled warmly at Chill, however. After the introductions,

126

Chill waited for Ozzie to explain his daughter's disappearance.

"We had an argument. She was angry. She ran out. Moses here said he saw her go into the woods about an hour or so ago."

"That right, Moses?" Tom asked.

"Yes suh. She run through thisaway. Lotta cottonmouths in deah."

"What are cottonmouths?" asked Kim.

"Poisonous snakes," Chill answered.

"Why in hell didn't you stop her, Moses?" asked Tom, a bitter edge to his tone.

"None of my business, suh. She ain't my gal."

"Tom, it's my fault." Ozzie's voice was strangely thick, low. "Let's fan out and call out for her. Maybe if she hears us looking for her, she'll come back. I don't think she meant to run away exactly. I think she was just looking for privacy and a place to think."

"Okay, Ozzie," said Tom, "you better stick close to Moses. He knows his way around. Hal, you stay here and wait in case she comes back. You're hardly dressed for the boonies. Chill, you search toward Moses' house, since you've been there. I'll cut through on an angle and circle back. Kim, you can stay close to me, okay? Moses and Ozzie can head toward the bluffs. That okay with you, Moses?"

"Yes suh, just fine. Be getting dark directly. I don't want to be around that place over deah at sunset."

"Where's that, Moses?" asked Chill. "Is that where the family plot is? The cemetery? The Grandier tomb?"

Moses nodded, his eyes rolling so that the whites showed.

"Come on, then, let's get started," said Tom. It shouldn't take long to find her, if she's willing to be found. She's probably sitting out there next to a tree right now, getting ready to come back in."

But she wasn't.

They heard her screams before any of them had taken a step.

# CHAPTER FIFTEEN

"Ginger!" Ozzie yelled, the sound wrenched from his throat, full of anguish.

"That's from over by the tomb, isn't it, Moses?" asked Tom.

The black man nodded somberly.

"Well, let's go find her!"

"Moses, can you lead us there?" asked Chill.

"I reckon."

"Come on, then, dammit!" from Ozzie. "My God, let's not just stand here!"

"Watch out for the snakes," Moses warned, trotting in the direction of the girl's screams.

The group followed the black man in a ragged run. He took a path into the thick of the woods. Tall pines and oaks blotted out the sun as they headed toward the bluffs they could not see. The ground was swampy in places. Moses skirted the damp spots. The screams died away, and silence settled over the group. Their footsteps thudded over the earth; their clothes scraped noisily against the underbrush. Shafts of sunlight filtered through the trees as the forest thinned.

"Ginger!" Ozzie called.

There was no answer.

"Christ! Where is she? Ginger!"

129

All but Moses were panting now and confused. The trees thinned out even more. Moses kept up his steady trot. He seemed tireless. His breathing was even, his long legs carrying him faster than the others despite the appearance of slowness. Chill had the feeling that Moses knew exactly where he was going. He hadn't faltered. He skirted the low places where dampness made the ground soggy. There was a stench of decay in the air, of rotting moss and stagnant water. It was humid.

"Ginger!" Breathless, Ozzie kept calling. His voice got weaker and weaker. Still, Moses loped on, never looking behind him, never wavering.

The black man broke into the open. The bluffs loomed ahead of them, yards away—limestone encrusted with vines and cracked with roots, scraggly trees gnarled by the wind and water, struggling for footing in the crevices.

Moses stopped in his tracks.

The others pulled up and surrounded him.

"Listen!" the old man said, raising his hand for silence.

Chill looked everywhere. His ears strained to hear. Something. Anything.

His eyes followed the movement of Moses' head. To the left, in what seemed to be an outcropping of rock, was the Grandier tomb. In a clearing in front of it, there were several mounds and tombstones. There were no crosses. Some of the ancient tombstones, gray, almost black where the granite had darkened, were tilted, with pieces chipped off. There were only a few of them, dominated by the massive sepulchre that had been blasted out of rock. Behind the tangle of ivy vines that crawled over the tomb, Chill could make out a door of massive steel. He knew the sepulchre was not that old, but already the vines had claimed it, spreading out over its face in all directions.

Chill looked at the grounds, seeking out footprints. He couldn't see any. Yet Ginger was here, somewhere.

They all heard it then. A low moan, coming from beyond the graveyard.

"Ginger, is that you?" Ozzie's voice quavered with fear. "We're here, honey. Where are you?"

They heard a watery sound. A faint splash, followed by another moan.

"Over there!" Chill said, pointing to the dark patch of woods beyond the small cemetery.

"Hold on," Moses said. "That drops off into swamp back over yonder. Lotta cottonmouth in deah."

"Maybe I'd better go in alone first," Chill said. ⎯

"I'll go with you," said Ozzie quickly. "It's gotta be her."

"Tom—you, Hal, and Kim wait here with Moses. I'll call you if I need you." Chill was already headed for the sounds they had heard. He threaded his way between the tombstones, glancing at the faded names etched in the stones. They were all French, meaningless to him.

Moses had been right. The land sloped off beyond the graveyard. Chill stopped to listen. Ozzie hovered at his elbow, holding his breath. He called to his daughter again.

An answer. "Daddy?"

"Over there!" Chill said, pointing off to his right. "Be careful. It's pretty steep here. And slimy."

Chill's shoes were quickly covered with muck as he went down the slope, hanging onto the brush and trees for support. He saw the skid marks and pointed them out to Ozzie.

"She must have slid down into that bog from here. It's treacherous."

"I see," said Ozzie. "I hope she's all right."

"She's alive."

There was more than a set of slide-marks on the bank, however. Chill saw marks where someone's foot had been, dug in sideways to keep from slipping. He kept this knowledge to himself.

"Stay here, Ozzie. I'll try to go down there. I may need some help getting back up."

"All right. Hurry."

Chill took the bank at a different angle. He didn't want to disturb the skid marks or the other tracks. He carefully worked his way to the left. It was dark, shaded from the sun by the tops of the tall trees. He let his eyes adjust to the light before he went too far down. He heard the sound of something slithering across the wet earth. There was a muffled splash deeper in the woods. Something scraped against the bark of a tree.

"Ginger? Can you hear me? Can you see me? It's Chill."

There was a gurgle, like someone gargling. A turtle? A water moccasin? A cottonmouth?

He hunched over, holding onto a tree branch for support. He saw that he was in a wide basin. A few more feet and he would be at the shallow edges of the stagnant, algae-covered water. He strained his eyes to see. Was Ginger here? Was there quicksand? Did it drop off into a hole?

"Dammit, Chill, do you see her yet?"

"Not yet. She can't be far from me, though."

"Ginger! Help us! We can't see you."

"Daddy?"

Chill saw her then. Just her head. He saw why he couldn't see her before. She was obviously on her back, her body entirely under the slimy water. Her face and hair, strands floating on the water, were visible above the water line. She looked like Ophelia.

"I see her, Ozzie. Stand by. Ginger, I'm coming to get you. Hold on."

"Y—yes?"

Chill followed the curve of the basin. He would have to pull her out by her hair unless he wanted to risk becoming mired in the muddy bottom of the stagnant pool. He pulled himself along by grasping the saplings higher up on the bank. He was sweating from the exertion and the dampness. His feet slipped several times, and he had to hold on tightly to keep from slipping in the mire. He could see Ginger more clearly now. Her mouth kept sliding under the green mass of organisms on the surface. It was an effort for her to hold her head above water. She appeared to be very weak from her struggles.

He heard a distant shout. It was Kim.

"Did you find her?"

"Tell her we did, Ozzie." Chill saw that he could reach the girl with his hands if he could find footing at the basin's far end. His trousers were soaked, muddy. The going was slow, but gradually he came to the point closest to her.

"I'm going to have to pull you out by your hair, Ginger," he said calmly. "Are your feet stuck in the bottom?"

She gurgled, her mouth half in the water.

"Y—yes," she managed.

"It's going to hurt some. I'm sorry."

He found a sapling and pulled on it, testing. It

133

held. If he could get her up on the bank, he could make his way out the other side. Perhaps there was surer footing there.

"Don't try to help me. Just relax if you can, Ginger. I'm going to pull you out, but if you struggle, it will make it more difficult. I know it's going to hurt some but it will only be for a little while. Now, don't say anything. Just relax."

He grasped her hair as close to her scalp as possible, making sure that several strands were in between each of his fingers. Her hair was wet, slick with slime. He gave the hair a half-twist and pulled. Ginger was a dead weight in the water.

Her head came up out of the water as he pulled, straining to lift at the same time. He needed both hands, but because of the precarious footing, he was unable to relinquish his grip on the sapling. His hand slipped on the strands of hair. He twisted some more, groaning with the effort.

Ginger whimpered from the pain at her scalp, yet he dared not stop pulling. Sweat began to drip from his forehead and under his arm. His stomach muscles tautened, the sinews in his arms stretched to the breaking point. He tugged, digging in his heels as best he could into the slippery bank. The sapling seemed about to tear loose from its mooring as he applied more and more pressure while he pulled. Ginger's feet seemed to be caught in a branch underwater. Finally, he felt her move his way. He bore down on the sapling as his other arm bent toward him.

"Have you got her?" Ozzie called in a fearful whisper.

Chill had no energy to answer. He changed his grip

on the sapling, moving his hand nearer its base. Ginger sank slightly, but he managed to keep her head above water. She moaned with the pain in her scalp, but was too exhausted to cry out any more. She was helpless and weak, so she did not struggle. Chill was grateful for that. His task was difficult enough without hysteria or animation complicating his tug-of-war.

He eased the soaked and frightened girl up on the bank.

"Don't move yet," he told her. "You might slide back into the water. I'm going to scoot you up on the bank. Don't try to help me."

He moved higher up on the bank, then leaned over, his legs straddling her arms. He put his hands under her armpits and pulled her toward him. He changed position again and repeated the maneuver. His breath came in short, staccato gasps now, but he knew the worst was over. In another few moments, he had her up on the bank. She looked up at him with wide, grateful eyes. Her jeans clung to her hips and legs. Ropes of slime festooned her body. Her T-shirt clung to her torso, the breasts and nipples outlined beneath, the white cotton of the shirt damp with green algae.

"She's out of the water," Chill called to her father. "Wait there. We'll come over." To Ginger, he asked, "Are you all right?"

She nodded her head quickly. Tears welled up in her eyes. Chill took out his handkerchief and dabbed her cheeks.

"You'll be fine. We'll get you up to the house. Don't try to talk yet, if you don't want to. It's been a pretty horrible experience for you."

The girl nodded.

"I'm going to try and carry you on to solid ground. Just relax; let me pick you up."

He bundled her up in his arms and made his way through the tangled brush, circling the basin carefully, testing every spot before he put his foot down. He let her legs slide out of his arms when they reached her father. But she was too weak to stand by herself. Chill had to support her. Ozzie threw his arms around her and drew her wet body to his. He was weeping, as well, patting the back of her head with his hand.

"I'm so sorry, darling," he said, soothingly. "Forgive me. I'll make it up to you, Ginger, baby. I'm just so glad you're safe."

"I—I'm sorry too, Daddy," she sobbed. "It was so—so horrible. I ran away and ended up in this swampland. I heard something behind me. I got scared. I ran. I fell into that awful pool of slime. It felt like somebody pushed me."

"Somebody pushed you?"

"I—I don't know," said Ginger, weakly. "It felt like it. But there was nobody there. I was so scared. I'd heard noises. I thought something, an animal, was after me. There were rats. And snakes."

"There now," said her father. "It's all over. Can you walk?"

"I don't know. My legs have no feeling in them."

Chill looked at her legs and feet. The flesh on her feet and toes was shriveled from being in the water so long. He bent down and began massaging her legs and feet.

"This might help your circulation," Chill said. "A hot bath will fix her up, Ozzie. We'll have Dr. Morgan take a look at her. Come on, Ginger, we'll carry you to where the others are waiting for us."

Ginger put her arms over the men's shoulders and, legs dangling, was carried out into the open. The trio was greeted enthusiastically by Kim and Hal, while Moses, dour and impassive, regarded them all from the background.

"We're so happy you're safe!" Kim exclaimed.

Chill introduced Hal to Ginger, who nodded feeble acknowledgment. Chill slipped her arm from his shoulder.

"Tom, help her and Ozzie get her back to the house. Hal, Kim—you go with them. I want to talk to Moses a minute and have a look around. You'll be okay, Ginger. I'll see you after a while."

"Th—thanks," she said. "I don't deserve such good treatment. You saved my life back there."

Chill gave her a wink and patted her cheek.

"I'm just glad you're safe," he said.

"She needs some brandy and milk," said Kim, smiling at the bedraggled girl.

"And dry clothes," added her father. He chuckled with the release of tension, put his arm around his daughter's waist and squeezed her warmly.

Ginger gave him a look of gratitude, laden with deeper meaning.

Tom put her other arm over his shoulder and grasped her waist with his other arm, wondering what had transpired between Ozzie and Ginger.

Chill looked at Moses. "You knew that girl was out here, Moses." It was a flat statement. There was a hard edge to Chill's voice.

"Not exactly." Moses' eyes moved like tormented beings in their sockets.

"You came straight to this tomb—this graveyard."

Moses shrugged.

137

"I want to know why. That girl was pushed into that basin."

Moses glanced around nervously. Chill speared him with an accusing glance, however, and didn't turn the uncomfortable man loose.

"Well?" Chill asked.

"I just figgered this a likely direction. Nobody out here, man."

Chill was disgusted.

"Come with me, Moses," he said. "I want to show you something."

Moses drew back, but Chill's shoulders tensed for action, and the black man knew that Chill was prepared to use force.

Chill went back to the basin. He pointed to the skid marks and the other set of footprints in the bank.

"Those aren't your footprints, Moses. They're too small. Someone else was out here. Someone tried to kill that girl and make it look like an accident. Or scare her to death. Now, you tell me who else was out here!"

"You barking up the wrong tree, man."

Savagely, Chill whirled on Moses. He grabbed him by the collar and drew his face close to his own.

"Damn you! I want answers," he growled. "You're hiding something, and I want to know what it is."

Chill was unprepared for the black man's response. His eyes blurted out tears that streamed unashamedly down his face.

"I—I can't, man, don't you understand? I don't wants to die."

Chill released his grip on the man's collar. Moses fell back on his haunches. He got up, slowly, a broken man. He turned his back on Chill and walked off dejectedly. His sobs made his shoulders go up and down in a mournful rhythm. Chill felt very sad. Someone had scared the black man. Scared him half to death.

He had to find out who that someone was. And soon!

# CHAPTER SIXTEEN

"Your hunch was right, Chill. Pope Gregory the Great was the key." Hal puffed on his pipe as he riffled through his attaché case. They were in Chill's room, chairs drawn up around his desk. The door was shut, locked from the inside.

"You mean Grandier was mentioned in the ancient literature?" Chill munched thoughtfully on a sesame stick. Laura leaned on the desk, looking up at both men, interested, as always, in their rapport, the way they dug at facts, behind facts, and into facts.

"The very name," smacked Hal with satisfaction. "Here, look at this." He drew out a few sheets of manuscript paper. Chill recognized the typing as Hal's. His *o*'s, *m*'s and *n*'s were filled in with ribbon ink. The *l* and the *h* jumped out of alignment. Hal loved his old Remington, however, even though he had a new electric Olympia 45.

Chill read what Hal had typed for him.

"This is from his *Dialogues*?" Chill asked.

Hal nodded, a plume of smoke curling upward from his pipe.

"Who was Pope Gregory the Great?" asked Laura. She had changed into tennis togs. Her sleek olive skin gleamed under the white garments. She wore a single turquoise amulet, a thunderbird, on a chain around her neck. Her black hair was tied back with a blue-green ribbon that matched the amulet. She loved jade and turquoise and alternated wearing jewelry with those stones.

"Gregory the Great," Hal said, "was Pope from 590 to 604. A strange bird. He wrote a lot about ecclesiastical matters, but harped mainly on the possession of man by devils. This guy was very superstitious."

"He was well-versed in miracles performed by the saints, too," Chill added. "Some of his material is confusing, especially the scraps of ancient writings that he collected."

"He got his authors mixed up most of the time," Hal added. "But literature was pretty dry in those days. Old Greg's stuff was about the most interesting to read, so his books survived."

"So, do you think what he has to say about Grandier is valid?" Laura asked.

"A good question," Hal said, running a hand through his short-cropped hair. "What do you think, Chill?"

"Could be. It's all we have to go on right now. You did a good job here, Hal," Chill said, studying Hal's extensive typewritten notes.

"What does he say, exactly?" Laura wanted to know.

"The section I typed up," Hal said, dealt with a curious situation in the old monastery of Loudun."

Chill leaned back in his chair and swallowed the last of his sesame stick.

"The genesis of that story, the one that concerns us here," Chill explained, "was related by Gregory in his *Dialogues*. It concerned a servant in a convent, who swallowed a devil. She had munched on some leaves of lettuce from the convent garden one day. Afterwards, she knew that she was possessed by a demon. An exorcist was called in, who railed at the devil to leave the poor girl's body. The devil left, saying that he didn't mean any harm. He had been minding his own business, perched quietly on the leaf of lettuce when the girl came up and swallowed him."

Laura and Hal chuckled at Chill's account.

"However, this little event preceded a whole series of incidents in nunneries involving possession, demons, devils, and horrible beasts."

"Nunneries," said Hal, "were prime places for such happenings. Gregory understood this, of course, since he was a stickler for rules and regulations. He knew the dangers of demons in such quarters."

"That's right." Chill warmed to his subject. "Convents were particularly susceptible to encroachment by devils. The rules were rigid, so demons were always on the lookout to test the weaknesses of the inhabitants. They stirred up long-repressed passions in the nuns and serving girls, the gardeners and cooks."

"I think Balzac must have read some of this stuff," Hal snorted.

"Right," said Chill. "He didn't ascribe the lusts and passions he wrote about to demons, but it's the same idea."

"I thought you said Loudun was a monastery," said Laura. "Doesn't that mean monks?"

"Monks and nuns too, in those days. I think monastery and nunnery were interchangeable terms, actually."

"So what happened at Loudun?"

"Nothing in Gregory's day," said Hal, "but Chill's mention of him put me on the right track. The Loudun story occurred in the late 1720s. By the way, Chill, what made you think of Pope Gregory?"

142

"Joan herself. She appeared to me to be in the type of swoon described by Gregory the Great and many others: the way she collapsed when Moses first pointed his finger at her. And the fact that Louisiana was predominantly French-settled, with Catholicism the main religion of the early inhabitants. Actually, a wild hunch, I guess."

Laura looked at both men and smiled warmly.

"You two," she laughed. "Is there anything you guys haven't read on occultism?"

"Yeah," said Hal. "Chill's next book."

"When I lived with my Uncle Martin in Vienna, I read through his library on the occult. He had quite a few volumes. Later, when he died, I acquired them. In the years between, I've tried to keep up with everything."

"Your Uncle Martin was a psychic, wasn't he?" asked Hal.

"I think so. During my stay, we participated in strange rites that he called 'raising the spirits.' I was scared half out of my wits most of the time. He lived in an old gothic house that was terrifying, without exaggeration. When he was dying, a few years ago, he told me that he had no fear of death. He believed that life would go on, in another dimension. I believed him, and I've spent my entire adult life trying to prove that Uncle Martin might have been right."

"I didn't know about him," Laura said. "You never told me about your Uncle Martin before."

Chill smiled.

"There are a lot of things I haven't told you."

Then she smiled and finally said it. "Maybe you'd like to tell me who you were with last night? It was Kim, wasn't it?"

"I think we'd better get back to the question of the Grandiers, Laura."

Laura pouted for a second, then reached over and patted his hand.

"Tell me about the Grandiers," she said. "We can talk about your private life some other time." She squirmed in her seat.

"Yeah," said Hal, "I'd like to know more about that too."

Chill drew back his arm as if to give Hal a karate chop across the nose. Hal grinned and ducked, his pipe grazing the edge of the desk.

"You two think you have me in a squeeze," Chill said, "but I really think this is more serious than any of us imagines."

"I'm sure it is," said Laura. "I looked in on Joan. She looks like a—a dead person. Only there's something marvelously alive about her. She's—she's a sleeping beauty. There's color in her cheeks; she doesn't look worried—she's at peace with the world."

Hal still had not seen Joan. Chill had promised to take him to her room later on. He wanted to talk to Tom and Morgan anyway, and he wanted Hal to be in on the conversation.

Having studied Hal's notes, Chill took over the storytelling. "It looks like Hal's research led him to Loudun. One of the nuns, a young woman, was strange, perhaps possessed by one of the little devils that Pope Gregory the Great wrote about. It says here this nun was known as Joan of the Angels."

Laura drew in her breath sharply.

Hal picked up the story. "She was the daughter of Baron Louis Bécier, who was a wealthy landowner of the time. The nunnery was poor, and Joan saw an opportunity there, since the Mother Superior was due to

144

leave the convent shortly. Joan wanted to take over as head of the convent. Joan's strategy was to appear as poor and humble as the other nuns, even though she had lived more extravagantly in the past. She put on a good act, since she was given the top job. Once in a position of authority, however, she reverted to type, living as she had been accustomed to before becoming a nun. She was, in her day, quite a swinger. And that's when Grandier came along," Hal added.

"Urbain Grandier was a priest," Chill said, reading out loud. "He was handsome, brilliant, gifted in several ways. In Loudun, he cut a wide swath, taking over as parish priest of the town. The ladies there flipped over him. He had ways of consoling widows and of comforting nervous maidens that were more secular than clerical.

"He made several enemies in Loudun, since he had seduced the daughter of Trincant, the king's attorney. Grandier went on from Trincant's daughter to Madeleine de Brou, according to Hal's report here, who was the daughter of the king's counselor. He wrote a naughty little essay condemning the policy of celibacy in the priesthood. News of this got out and created another scandal."

"He sounds like one of Balzac's characters at that," Laura said.

"Well, maybe he was," said Chill. He wiped his forehead where beads of perspiration had started to form.

"Go on," said Laura. "I'm fascinated."

Chill looked down at the papers again, paraphrasing Hal's notes as he read quickly. "Joan of the Angels was intrigued and fascinated by Grandier, whom she'd never met, and by the wild stories about him and his exploits. She saw him as one of God's most radiant angels. Instead of speaking to her like an angel, however, he made some obscene suggestions. This was never proven, of course."

"I see," said Laura. She seemed to be looking backward in time. She leaned back, her face falling in shadow as she drew away from the circle of lamplight. She fluffed her blouse. It had begun to stick to her skin. She, too, was perspiring.

"Anyway, the old prior of the convent, a monk named Moussant, died at that time. Joan offered the position to Urbain Grandier. He refused the job. That seemed to upset her. Her psychic disturbances worsened, and the nightly hush of the convent was often disrupted by her hysterical screams. Because she couldn't control her emotions, she felt that this was a sign of moral weakness. She became a strict disciplinarian with herself and ordered the nuns to whip her mercilessly."

Laura gasped.

"She sounds weird to me," she said. "Perhaps a masochist."

"A leather freak, most probably," Hal said irreverently.

"The whippings apparently stirred up some inner yearnings of the other nuns, as well. They soon began to suffer psychic upheavals. Several of them began to suffer hallucinations about Grandier, just like Joan. One of them, referred to as the Dampierre nun, became important later. She was very close to Joan.

"Joan realized she had unleashed some powerful forces in the convent. She couldn't handle it herself. So she enlisted the aid of Canon Mignon, a relative of the king's solicitor, Trincant. Between them, they decided that Mignon should look into the situation very carefully."

"The plot thickens," Hal said.

"Or sickens," quipped Laura.

"For sure," said Chill. "Those who were out to nail Grandier recalled that a priest in Marseilles was burned alive at the stake for having bewitched a young *fille*. They thought that Grandier might just qualify for similar justice. Exorcists were sent out to the nunnery by high officials of the court. The nuns were forced to witness the strange rites, the hypnotizing chants used to exorcise demons. Joan went into convulsions, convinced that the devils mentioned by Gregory infested her and everyone else at the nunnery. Her own possession was contagious apparently. Like flies, nuns fell into fits, uttering meaningless sounds, unintelligible gibberish. The Dampierre nun in particular kept shouting the name 'Grandier' over and over again."

"Sounds like a madhouse," Laura said, moving closer to the desk again.

"It's hot in here," Hal said, dabbing with a handkerchief at perspiration streaming down his face.

Chill got up from the chair and checked the windows. There was steam on the insides of them. He opened them wide but felt no breeze. The air from outside was fetid with the cloying stench of decaying vegetation, warm like the blast from a furnace. The moon was not yet up, and it was pitch dark outside. Silent.

"Hot night," he said, coming back to his chair.

"Don't leave me in suspense," Laura said. "What happened next?"

"Grandier's enemies accused him of having bewitched the nuns. Their arguments were pretty convincing. It was then that Grandier realized the extent of the plot against him. He made an appeal to the

147

bailiff of Loudun, begging to have the nuns put away. The exorcists, however, didn't obey the bailiff's orders to isolate the nunnery."

"I imagine they were getting their kicks out there," said Hal.

"Yes, they had power over a bunch of screaming, squirming nuns. Grandier then went to the archbishop of Bordeaux, who sent his personal physician, Dr. Sourdis, to examine the nuns. He declared that they were not possessed, so the archbishop ruled out further exorcism rituals and ordered the nuns to be confined to their rooms. This calmed the general hysteria for a while. Later on, however, the convulsions and shrieking began again. Sourdis reported that the nuns 'were persecuted constantly by impure temptations.' They scurried about, led by Joan and her friend, the Dampierre nun, begging for the flesh of Urbain Grandier. This time, their entreaties could not be ignored."

"Doesn't Tom have air conditioning in this place?" Laura was fanning her face with her hand.

"I doubt it," replied Chill. "I haven't seen a thermostat since I've been here."

"It wasn't that warm today," Hal said.

"Must be the humidity," Laura told them. She stood up, stretched her arms, and pulled her damp clothing away from where it had stuck to her body.

"Maybe we can take a swim after a while." Chill realized that he, too, was dripping with perspiration. A warning bell sounded in the recesses of his brain. He tried to isolate it, but the story before him drew him back. "Let's get on with this. I'll be as brief as I can."

"Yes, hurry. That pool sounds good to me." Laura

withdrew from the lamp once again as if even its heat was too much to bear.

"The Counselor of State, Laubardemont, came to Loudun to assess the situation. He was a hard, arrogant man. His motto was, 'Give me two lines written by a man—and I will hang him.' He was also personally involved in the situation. He was related to Joan of the Angels and the brother-in-law of the Dampierre nun. The Counselor was impressed with the horror of the situation. He sent his report to Cardinal Richelieu, who promptly ordered Grandier's arrest. Grandier, in 1618, had written a libelous diatribe against Richelieu, so the time for revenge was at hand.

"The exorcists went back to work, not only at the convent, but at the churches in Loudun. Everything was now out in the open. Father Gault led the attack on the demons and managed to exorcise a few. I think what's important, though, is the document that Gault made the exorcised nuns sign. This one was written by Joan of the Angels: *I promise that when leaving this creature, I will make a slit below her heart as long as a pin, that this slit will pierce her shirt, bodice, and cloth, which will be bloody. And tomorrow, on the twentieth of May at five in the afternoon, I promise that the demons Gresil and Amand will make their opening in the same way, but a little smaller— and I approve the promises made by Leviatam, Behemot, Beherie with their companions to sign, when leaving, the register of the church St. Croix! Given the nineteenth of May, 1629. It's signed, Asmodeus.*"

"That document still exists," said Hal. "It's in the Bibliothèque Nationale in Paris."

"To make a long story short," continued Chill, "another document that was found was the convincing

149

factor in Grandier's guilt. It was a pact with Lucifer, signed by him, countersigned by Beelzebub, Satan, Elimi, Leviathan, and Astaroth. Joan of Angels was found ~~to~~ be possessed by the demon of lust, Iscaaron. Grandier ultimately underwent agonizing and horrendous tortures at the hands of the Capuchin Tranquille. The man showed absolutely no mercy. He was not a nice man. And in spite of Grandier's pleading, Capuchin Tranquille had him burned at the stake in 1634 before cheering crowds. Joan died a holy death many years later in 1665.

"Wow!" exclaimed Laura. "That's very heavy stuff."

"It gives us something to go on," said Chill.

"That date," said Laura. "May 20th, wasn't it?"

"That's right," said Chill. "And May 20th is Joan Brunswick's birthday."

# CHAPTER SEVENTEEN

Hal gave a low whistle. His pipe had gone out.

The temperature upstairs in the house inexplicably rose to over 100 degrees.

"I can hardly breathe," Laura announced, rushing to the window near Chill's bed. "It's stifling in here."

"I'm going to change into tennis clothes myself," said Chill.

"Good idea," said Hal. "If I can just remember where my room is."

"Next to mine, the last one on the left," Laura said.

"I'll have to check on Joan," Chill told Laura after he'd changed. "Morgan's probably having a fit."

"Wait a minute, before you go," Laura said. "What do you think of all that data on Grandier and Joan of the Angels? Do you honestly think there's a connection here?"

Chill finished tying his shoelaces and joined Laura by the window. At least there was an illusion of coolness there. He looked at her thoughtfully for a long moment before replying.

"I think there's a definite connection. There are too many similarities. In the names, especially. It looks to me like Patty's uncle has had his eye on Joan ever since she was born. If my hunch is correct, this is the

151

strangest case of reincarnation I've ever heard of or seen."

"Do you think Joan knew about it before?"

"No. I still think she's an innocent. In fact, the thing that bothers me about this case is that there has been no hysteria, no evidence of any mental disorders in Joan's history."

"Reincarnation I can buy, but does that mean that Joan is following some preordained path of destiny?"

Before he could reply, Hal returned, dressed in cut-off army fatigues and T-shirt. Laura started giggling when he came in. His bony white legs protruded from well-worn leather slippers. He carried his pipe, pouch, and lighter in one hand. He fanned himself with a copy of *Vegetarian Times*.

"Maude Ryerson sent this along with me," he told Chill. "Makes a fair fan."

"If you keep fanning it like that, it'll be in shreds before I can read it," Chill said, laughing.

"You look like a beach bum," Laura teased.

"I am, at heart."

"Chill was talking about the case," she said seriously. "I just asked him if he thought that Joan of the Angels was reincarnated as Joan and whether he thought her fate was preordained."

"Reincarnation?" Hal asked. "Why now? Why here?"

"We may never know," said Chill. "It's unusual for someone to be reincarnated into the same family. However, Urbain Grandier was burned alive. Some karmic flaw could be involved here. I do know that the Grandiers were from France—from a place called Loudun."

"Holy shit!" exclaimed Hal.

"Exactly. That's convincing enough. Let's work on

this theory for a moment. Say that Joan of the Angels was a factor in Urbain Grandier's death. Say he wanted revenge, needed to work out the karmic debt for both of them. Maybe it's taken a complicated route through the centuries to get to this particular point in time. Now, Joan Brunswick is the reincarnation of Joan of the Angels. Grandier, the great-uncle, is Urbain. Maybe he's lived through numerous reincarnations trying to work out the correct path toward a reunion. Or maybe he planned it as a double reincarnation so that history itself would be satisfied."

"But her great-uncle's dead!" Laura forgot the heat in the room. Her dark eyes blazed with an intensity that matched Chill's own.

"Yes, he's dead. That's what bothers me about it," admitted Chill. "I don't have all the answers, Laura. That's why I think you might have to enter into a trance. Do you think you could make contact with Grandier himself? Or with someone who knows about all this?"

Laura wet her lower lip and pushed it upward until it covered her upper lip. "It's difficult to say what I might find out. I could try."

"It might be dangerous. Hal and I would have to watch you pretty closely. We're dealing with demons here. Perhaps one called Iscaaron. Perhaps the whole hierarchy."

"I understand," she said soberly.

"Good. Tonight, then, after everyone's asleep. I feel time is running out on us. Joan's birthday is Sunday, the 20th. This is Friday, which doesn't leave us much time."

Hal started to fill his pipe, then thought better of it. He looked as if he'd just come from a sauna. His clothes were soggy and wrinkled. Beads of sweat

153

trickled through the short hairs of his scalp and onto his forehead. He had to wipe his eyebrows constantly to keep the moisture from dripping into his eyes.

"What does that girl, Ginger, have to do with all this?" Hal asked.

Chill gave him a sharp look.

"Very astute question, my friend. She's another clinker in this deal. Another big X. When I found her out by the old graveyard, there were tracks other than hers over there. They didn't belong to Moses either. They were small, but I'd say, offhand, they were a man's. He probably wasn't a very strong man."

"A dwarf's?" Hal put his pipe in his mouth anyway—from habit.

"No, bigger than that. A small man. Ginger said she felt someone push her. Right now, I have no answers on where Ginger Branson fits into all this. Whoever pushed her, though, was human. I think Moses knows who it was."

"Moses? Why, he seems so nice, so harmless." Laura wasn't prepared to accept Chill's evaluation of the black man.

"Moses looks to me like a man under pressure," Chill said. "He may not want to know who pushed Ginger. But I'm sure he does. He may be a pawn in this. I think he's scared out of his mind. I also think he's scared of two things: the man who tried to do Ginger in, and the evil we're after out here."

"Well, I feel sorry for him," said Laura.

"I do too," Chill admitted. He looked at his watch. "Let's go. The heat's becoming unbearable here. I don't think it's natural. Let's see if it extends throughout the house. I've got to check on Joan, too."

"I had a short talk with Patty while you all were

out looking for that girl. She's worried about Joan, and Tom, as well," Laura said.

The upper hallway didn't seem to be as warm as Chill's room. He tapped quietly on Joan's door. It opened a moment later.

Bernice Baines peered at them suspiciously. Her uniform was limp and wrinkled.

"I'll have to ask the doctor if the three of you can come in," she said. The door closed. Several seconds later it reopened. "All right," she said. "But I warn you, it's awful hot in here."

"We know," said Laura, smiling at the nurse.

Morgan looked worried, but he managed a scowl at Chill. He dabbed at his own forehead with a handkerchief. Mrs. Baines resumed taking Joan's pulse, her chair pulled up close to the bed. Tom's clothes hung loosely on him. Patty was wearing a sunsuit and held Tom's hand in hers as she gazed at her daughter's calm face.

"Pulse the same. Temp's unchanged," said Mrs. Baines.

"She's the only one who's cool here," Morgan muttered. "I still think she should be in a hospital."

Tom looked at Chill. Chill shook his head.

"I don't think you have to worry about Joan's health, doctor," Chill said evenly.

"What's that supposed to mean?" snapped Morgan.

"Just that I don't think this is a medical problem. You can't raise her pulse, or her temperature. She doesn't respond to any exterior stimulus. Am I right?"

"I grant you that," said Morgan begrudgingly. "It sure does beat anything I've ever seen."

"What are you getting at, Chill?" Tom asked. "Suppose you segue right into it."

"Joan's condition has nothing to do with any dis-

155

ease or medical syndrome. She isn't affected by this heat as we are, I notice. She's not perspiring. We are. Her stability is controlled, but not by anything you or I are doing. But I still can't explain it. You'll just have to trust me."

"Trust you?" Patty said. "Why should we? What are you keeping from us?"

"Easy now, Patty," Chill said soothingly. "I'm not trying to be mysterious. It's just that I don't have all the facts. I think you have enough to worry about without listening to my theories. I'm sure Dr. Morgan doesn't want to hear them either."

"I do," said Tom. "I backed you up before on the matter of the I.V. solution. Stan thinks you're wrong. Patty's undecided. This house is a goddamned oven. The Bransons are upset over Ginger and wanted to leave tonight. I asked them to stay until morning. We've got all kinds of problems here, and I think you're holding out on us."

"Okay, Tom," Chill said. "You and I'll talk. Then, if you think I ought to tell Patty and everyone else what I think, I will. Fair enough?"

Tom looked questioningly at Patty.

"It's all right with me," she said sourly, "although I resent being left out. We're talking about our daughter, Tom. I think I should be included in Chill's talk with you."

"I'm sure Chill wants to tell you, Patty," said Laura, "but he would rather wait until he checks some more things out. That's the way he works, you know."

Slightly mollified, Patty released Tom's hand.

"Go ahead, Tom. Talk to *your* friend. I'll stay here."

"Good idea, Patty," Chill said. "I think Joan's in danger and should be watched. I just don't think she'll die or that she is ill in any normal way—if there

156

is a normal way to be ill." He turned to Morgan. "I respect you, and I know you're trying to work on Joan as if she were a normal patient. But I'm afraid of any fungus getting into her bloodstream, any foreign material invading any of her bodily orifices."

"You seem pretty sure of yourself, Chillders." Morgan took his stethoscope from around his neck and laid it on the table beside the oscilloscope. "Are you saying that this condition is psychosomatic?"

"I don't want to bandy terms with you, Dr. Morgan. In a way, it's psychosomatic. But it wasn't induced by Joan herself. At least not consciously. And I don't think she's in any discomfort. Do you?"

"She doesn't appear to be," said Morgan.

"I wonder, doctor, if I might discuss a couple of examples of a similar nature with you."

"Go right ahead."

"Did you happen to read about the eighteen-year-old Michigan student who was trapped in a submerged car in a frozen pond for thirty-eight minutes?"

"I heard about it."

"He was pronounced dead at the scene. Then, as he was being put into the ambulance, he gave a kind of gasp. They worked on him, and he came back to life. Two weeks later, he was back in college."

"What's that got to do with Joan?" asked Patty.

"Well, nothing, perhaps. Except that this wasn't the only case of a drowning where the victim recovered. There are at least fifteen documented cases. The water temperature in each case was below 70 degrees Fahrenheit. They're known as 'cold-water drownings.' All but a few of these victims were revived successfully without permanent brain damage. I think this shows a survival factor previously undiscovered in humans."

"I fail to see the point here," Morgan said testily.

"Give me a moment more, doctor." Chill wiped his forehead. Everyone's eyes, including Mrs. Baines's, were riveted on him. "A doctor at the University of Michigan Medical Center, Nemiroff, looked into these cases."

"Martin Nemiroff?"

"Yes. Martin J. Nemiroff. He concluded that what saved these people who drowned in cold water was activation of an automatic response in mammals, which he called the 'diving reflex.' This works with the coldness of the water. The reflex slows the heartbeat and restricts the flow of blood to the skin, muscles, and other tissues less vulnerable to damage from the loss of oxygen."

"So the rest of the oxygen is directed to the heart and brain," added Morgan.

"Yes. The cold water, apparently, reduces the tissues' need for oxygen."

"You're saying that Joan's case is similar, Chill?"

Chill walked over to Joan's bed and looked down at her. He placed a hand on her cheek. She was as serene as a sleeping child. The others, curious, watched him.

"I'm saying we're just beginning to learn about human survival. Joan's dropping temperature bears a similarity to the survival technique they're calling the 'diving reflex.' Her body needs little fuel now. Her brain slows down in proportion to her body's heat. There is blood and oxygen in her brain, but just enough to keep it alive. The electrical output is low, so it needs little energy."

"I see," said Tom. "You're saying that Joan is like that kid who drowned. Some mechanism of survival has taken over, keeping her alive until she can be revived."

"That's right, Tom. I think our problems with Joan are going to come when she's awake. That's why I think she needs very careful and constant attention from now on."

"She's being watched constantly," said Morgan.

"I mean at least two people on duty here at all times. A nurse could go to the bathroom. Joan's temperature could rise, she could awaken and . . ."

"And what?" Patty startled them all with her querulous voice.

Chill smiled at her, glad that he had aroused her interest.

"I'd just watch her vital signs a lot more closely," said Chill. "This sudden rise in room temperature has me worried. It could mean that Joan is going to be awakened soon. Perhaps tonight. I want to be called in here as soon as she does."

Patty, Tom, and Dr. Morgan exchanged glances. There was still the question of authority between them.

"I think we could do that," said Morgan, heading off an unpleasant confrontation. "So you think the rising temperature is significant. I'll admit it's unbearably hot tonight."

"Yes, and I think Joan will start to come out of her hibernation soon."

"You're still calling this—this condition—hibernation." Morgan's voice still held a note of puzzlement, but he seemed more receptive to Chill's ideas now than before. He seemed willing to grant Chill some respect, after all.

"Have you ever heard of the Kleine-Levin syndrome, Dr. Morgan?" Chill riveted his gaze on the doctor's.

"Yes. I thought of it, in fact, in Joan's case."

"Good. So did I, but I'm not locked into that theory. Rather, I think this is a natural state Joan's in. Hibernation, if you will. Induced, I don't know how. So the distinction is important. I think Joan definitely is in a state similar to hibernation. The room was cold at first. Now it's warm. I think she's going to come out of that state very soon."

"I'd like to pursue this further," Morgan said. "Privately, I think. You've raised a lot of interesting questions in my mind."

"And some doubts?"

"And some doubts, Dr. Chilllders." The respect was there. The others in the room seemed to breathe a sigh of relief.

"Dr. Morgan," Chill said, "there's a quote that I memorized a long time ago, when I got into the field of parapsychology. It has helped me to keep an open mind. I wonder if you've ever read it. William James wrote it in *The Will to Believe.* 'Round about the accredited and orderly facts of every science there over floats a sort of dust-cloud of exceptional observations of occurrences minute and irregular and seldom met with, which it always prove more easy to ignore than to attend to. . . . Anyone will renovate his science who will steadily look after the irregular phenomena. And when the science is renewed, its formulas often have more of the voice of the exceptions in them than of what were supposed to be the rules.' "

"I have read that, Dr. Chilllders. I regret that I seem to have forgotten that particular quote."

Chill smiled.

"I forget to apply it myself, a lot of times. That's why I memorized it."

The tension in the room eased. Tom looked at Morgan and winked, pleased that the two men had come to some sort of understanding.

"Come on, Chill," Tom said. "Let's get to that talk, whatdaya say?"

"I'll wait here with Joan," said Patty. "I want to be here in case she wakes up. I'm sure Mrs. Dailey has supper on, something cool, if anyone's interested. I thought we'd just all eat as we wanted to tonight. Nothing formal."

"I'm famished," said Laura. "Come on, Hal, take me to dinner."

"You're on," said Hal.

The foursome left Joan's room and went downstairs. The heat, they noticed, greeted them there, as well.

# CHAPTER EIGHTEEN

It was cooler outside than inside the house.

Chill and Tom sat on the veranda in squeaky wicker chairs. Tom had built himself a tall drink, but only sipped at it. It was more a prop than a necessity. The night was clear, the sky sequined with stars. The moon had not yet risen, but light from the den filtered onto the veranda. The two men sat in silence for a while, enjoying the comparative coolness. The scents of magnolia and wisteria hung on the still air, mingled with the faint wisps of aroma from honeysuckle blossoms that had closed up for the night. Every so often, Tom slapped at a vagrant mosquito. They didn't seem to bother Chill. He claimed it was his vegetarian diet.

Ginger's going to be all right," Tom said, finally. It was not the opening that Chill had expected, but it was a welcome one.

"Yes. You got off the track there."

"It was inevitable. I just hope Patty doesn't do a freeze frame on me. I'm over it."

"She understands. Wasn't it Pirandello who remarked how tragic it would be to judge a man by a single isolated incident in his life? Stooping over to pick up a cigarette butt, or scratching his behind?"

162

"Dylan Thomas, too. Falling down the stairs drunk on a Sunday morning."

Both men laughed, and more of the tension from upstairs eased.

"What is it, Tom? Show biz?"

"It's more of a scramble than ever. I thought coming out here would give me some perspective. New Orleans was a good base. Some good talent there. Costs are going up so fast, though. It's harder to find space on the tube. I'm competing against cheap reruns of 'Lucy,' 'The Beverly Hillbillies,' and 'Andy Griffith.' "

"Yes. How about the public broadcasting stations?"

"A mortally wounded child with its tin cup out. No, it's more than a question of space. The hottest producer around uses data processing to come up with ideas. He makes G-rated films and cleans up. Not a swear word or a hooker in any one of them. Antiseptic. On the other hand, you have network censors asking you to 'please murder the baby tastefully,' or 'please see to it that the woman in the story is raped without offending accepted decorum.' Or 'please do not sensationalize the dead gopher,' if you're doing an outdoor flick. The last one I didn't make up, dammit!"

"You've got projects in the works?"

"Several. All of them good ones, Chill. I think violence is probably as obscene, if it's gratuitous, as sexual exploitation. But cleaning up violence is also obscene. Police shows on television show people being shot and killed. But they leave out the pain, the horror of a bullet hole in a man's chest or in his guts, and the blood. There has to be a middle ground. I also object to the so-called nature shows on television that don't show the real wilderness as it was, a terrible place, alien to man."

163

"What are you trying to do, then?"

"Make syndicated programs for television that are honest. Drama-docs, I call them. The truth in dramatic form."

"Like 'The Search for Noah's Ark?'"

"That was well done. The problem is that television is not a medium that lends itself to imparting information of a complex nature. It's an advertising medium. It's a way to hit people between the eyes to get them to buy a product or to work at them sublimally."

"Can you work around it, then?"

"I don't know, Chill. God knows I'm trying. I'm compromising, too."

"We all do that."

"Like Dr. Morgan." It had come around to that.

"Maybe, without realizing it. He's found himself in two worlds." Chill told him, then, about the research that Hal Strong had done on Grandier. Tom didn't say a word throughout the entire account. He sipped at his drink occasionally.

"I don't think Patty could handle this," he said when Chill was finished.

"Neither do I. Not right now. That's why I wanted you to know what I think first. She's worried about you right now. And about Joan."

"About the Ginger business . . . my drinking. Patty's a good woman, Chill. You know that. She's like Morgan, though. She doesn't stray very far from convention."

"That's what I like about you, Tom. You do."

"And I'm in trouble because of it," he laughed. "Look, Chill, I'll be frank with you. I've been hitting the bottle out here because I'm too far away from the action. Patty wanted to live here. I thought it would work out. It hasn't."

"Move back. You've still got a place in Beverly Hills or Malibu, haven't you?"

"I hate to give up. It's not my nature."

Chill stood up.

"When this is over, I think you'll want to leave the Grandier mansion far behind."

Tom rose from his chair. It squeaked as it released his weight.

"Hell, I want to leave here now. Cut to 'Exterior Los Angeles, Day, Long Shot.'"

"Coming in, Tom? I have some things to do. You should eat something."

"Later. I'm not hungry now. I just want to think about some things."

"See you in the morning, then—unless something comes up concerning Joan. I want to help."

"You've already helped a lot. You know, you ought to talk to Stan Morgan about Patty's uncle sometime . . . about his death."

"I intend to, Tom. In fact, I already know something about Grandier's death."

"You do?" Tom looked at Chill closely, then grinned. "I'm not surprised. It's hard to keep up with you."

"Good night."

He left him there. Tom walked to the stone railing at the edge of the veranda and peered out over the expanse of lawn. The garden was out there, dark and neglected. Patty's garden. Even as he looked, though, the moon started to rise. He thought he heard something stirring out there, in the direction of the bluffs. But he wasn't sure. He swirled the drink in his glass. The last ice cube clinked softly against the edge of the glass. Frowning, he tossed the drink out over the railing. He took a deep breath and seemed to stand taller. He waited for the moon to show its silver face over the tops of the frost-dusted trees.

The phone was ringing when Chill entered his room. He ran to it, jerking the instrument out of its cradle.

"Chill here," he said, out of breath.

"Damn, I've been ringing you for hours." It was Rudy Kellerman in Atlanta.

"Rudy! What have you got for me?"

"Where'd you get that stuff, Chill?"

"Never mind that, Rudy. You have any trouble checking it out?"

Rudy Kellerman was a precise man. He was also a thinker. His work at the Atlanta Center for Disease Control often involved exotic scientific exploration. His specialty was toxins, but he was a brilliant biologist who loved nothing more than a problem. He was at home with a microscope, hunched over a set of slides. He had contributed a number of important papers at scientific conventions, and his work appeared frequently in medical and scientific journals. He and Chill had known each other for about five years. They were neighbors. Like Chill, Rudy was a vegetarian and an amateur botanist. He always told Chill that he "knew too damn much about meat processing" to be anything else. Also like Chill, he loved plant life.

"No trouble," the scientist replied, "but I have to know something first. Before I tell you what I found out."

"Regulations?"

"Regulations. Was this stuff involved in any illness? If so, was it endemic or epidemic? Where exactly did you get it? I won't even ask you why you want to know. How's that?"

"Very gentlemanly of you, Rudy. No, it's not involved in any illness. So that's all the answer you get."

"Swell. You're a nice guy, Chill, even if you are a peanut-eater."

"You're an irreverent bastard yourself, Kellerman. Now, what's in that slime I sent you?"

"Well, I wouldn't eat it, that's for sure. Actually, it has the appearance and many of the properties of green algae, subkingdom Thallophyta. Since you're in Louisiana, I'd say this stuff probably came from a swamp. It grows on moist surfaces usually—turtle backs, banks of lakes and streams, at the base of trees. Food for fish. Most of the algae in this batch had flagella so that they could move independently. You probably don't want the technical terms right now, do you?"

"No, just the bottom line, thanks."

"The bottom line is that the species here didn't break down as it should have. The cell walls contained little or no cellulose and no storage of food as starch. I put some of them in a saucer with a starch compound, and the little microscopic devils devoured the food. Hungry little devils. Also, some green algae reproduce both asexually and sexually. Some are entirely asexual. Others have only sexual reproduction. In some kinds, the life cycle includes two different plant forms. Algae are basic to evolution, I feel—that is, most algae of this type."

"You're getting at something important, Rudy. Let's have it."

"Okay. These are asexual spores. Reproduction can occur from a single parent. These particular ones are avid breeders. From the way they performed on the slides, I made a conclusion or two. Number one is that they used their own food to reproduce rapidly, far more rapidly than algae—that is, normal algae—do. Yet the parents did not die. Emptied of their food storage, they kept searching for more. I experimented with a drop or two of fresh blood in the saucer. I wouldn't usually do this, but one of my technicians had a cut on his hand, and the algae had started reproducing there. We had to use a strong antibiotic to kill the spores."

"Were they trying to impregnate his blood stream?"

"How in hell did you know?"

"Just a little conclusion of my own, Rudy," Chill said drily. "Go on."

"All right. So I pricked my finger and let the blood drip onto the saucer. The action was amazing. We transferred some algae to a slide and repeated the process. The algae reproduced rapidly and displaced the blood. The end results were dinoflagellates, which are closely related to golden algae, another species. As near as I can determine on such short notice, these resembled *Gymnodinium brevis*, the kind of dinoflagellate that causes the 'red tides' that destroy sea life, that poison oysters and clams. A very strange occurrence in the laboratory, my friend."

"Yes, I see. You say you used an antibiotic to kill the spores?"

"Yes. Tetracycline. I feel certain, however, that the algae could overcome the effects of this in a few generations. The way the algae reproduced and changed from one *species to another*, however, makes me wonder if I shouldn't come down there and declare the whole area a disaster zone."

Chill sucked in a deep breath. Rudy was a persistent investigator. His academic pulse had quickened over the algae's behavior, his scientific libido had been tickled. He could picture Rudy on the other end of the line: balding, thin, moustachioed, looking somewhat like a cross between Karl and Groucho Marx (an intensity there in his eyes, and a mischievousness, too), his lab coat too small for him, his huge arms extending out of too-short sleeves, a mass of hair on his truck-driver's wrists. Rudy was a magnet for younger colleagues, who worshipped him.

Chill explained him to Hal once as a "variant of the second law of thermodynamics, which makes others' natures flow outward to fill in areas of lesser potential." Rudy was a bulldog when he tackled a problem. His enthusiasm tended to follow that law of thermodynamics. It was a powerful force, and Chill didn't want it unleashed right now.

"Rudy, thanks for looking into this for me. I don't want it to go any further. It's a freak of nature. What you looked at doesn't even exist any more." Chill's fingers were crossed as he said this to his friend.

"Are you up front with me?"

"Rudy, drop by my place and have Maude break out a bottle of plum wine. I made a batch six months ago that's matured by now. Tell her I sent you."

"You bastard. You're bribing me!"

"Good night, Rudy. Thanks."

He hung up the phone over Rudy's spluttering protests. He realized then that he was drenched with perspiration. Some of it was because of the heat in the room.

He changed clothes again and was going out the door, when he ran into the arms of Kim.

"I've been looking all over for you," she said.

"What's up?"

"Joan's room. Hurry. They said to get you."

169

"What's going on?"

"I don't know," she said. "Some change in her condition, I think. One of the nurses grabbed me as I was going by her room. Said to get you."

Kim was wearing tennis clothes, too, but her hair was wet.

"Been swimming?" he asked.

"Yes. The Bransons are still out by the pool. It's too hot in this damned house."

Chill knocked on the door to Joan's room. Francine Arnold opened the door a few seconds later.

"I'm sorry," she said. "Just Chill can come in."

"Oh, what the hell. Kim's messenger service. That's all I am around here."

Chill pecked her on the cheek.

"Don't start feeling sorry for yourself," he said. "I'll see you when I can."

He went in, then, hating to leave Kim out of it. The first thing he noticed was that Patty was clutching her daughter's hand. Dr. Morgan and the two nurses stood around Joan's bed, their faces grim and drawn with worry, puzzlement.

"What's happened?" Chill asked.

"Oh, Chill, she's—she's moving," cried Patty. "She moved. She—her pulse is getting stronger."

"Is that true?" Chill directed his question to Morgan.

"I think Patty's hopes are premature," he said sternly. "There's a slight increase in the pulse rate. It could be only a spasm. Her temperature has risen slightly."

"That's good, isn't it, Chill? Stan, it is a good sign, isn't it?"

Chill nodded in Morgan's direction, deferring the reply to him.

"It's a sign of a possible change," Morgan said cautiously.

Patty looked at Chill with eyes full of pleading. She kneaded her daughter's hand like a piece of dough, turning it over and over in her own hand. Her eyes were red-rimmed from crying. Her mouth trembled with the effort to contain her enthusiasm, her boundless hope.

"That's not all," she said, her eyes widening. "She spoke."

"What?" Chill asked. "She said something?" His eyes went to Morgan's for confirmation.

"None of the rest of us heard it," Morgan said. "I think Patty is working herself up into an emotional state that could be harmful."

"Never mind that," Chill said, suddenly disgusted with Morgan again. "Did you hear Joan say something, Patty?"

"Yes, I did," she said, sobs breaking through to her voice.

"What did she say?"

"She called out your name. And something else. Iscariot, I think. I heard it distinctly."

Chill felt his scalp prickle, the hairs on the back of his neck rise like cilia.

*Iscaaron.* That's what Joan must have said.

# CHAPTER NINETEEN

*Something snapped way back in her brain.*

*It sounded like a twig breaking. In her mind it was a footstep padding stealthily out of the darkness. No, not that. Not exactly. More like two fingers popping. A fingersnap. Of warning?*

*No. Attention. That was it.*

*There had been no consciousness of time before. Now there was—as if the snapping had set off an unseen clock. She could almost hear it ticking. Yet there was no such sound.*

*Something inside her mind opened, though.*

*A tiny door, way back there.*

*Then, the voices again. People speaking in whispers.*

*Heat, too. Warmth.*

*Very distant. Pervading.*

*Suffocating.*

*Something stirring. A hidden root. Probing, sensitized. Not painful yet, but like the tingling in a frostbitten toe as it warms up.*

*The giant cells of the brainstem began to decrease their activity. The flow of mediating acetylcholine finished off the dreams, letting the cerebral cortex awaken. The sounds separated and became distinct.*

*The whispers, like tufts of shredded cotton, reformed into solid wads, thick words.*

*Yet the cortex floated in its own calm sea, still, an island in the consciousness. The body was still on low power, its chemistry held to a minimum. Gradually, however, the pulse increased, the blood, once sluggish, quickened its flow. The heat responded.*

*A fear attached itself to the neuron flow. A smothering claustrophobia enveloped her weak consciousness.*

*She was still a prisoner.*

*And someone—something—was coming for her.*

*Iscaaron.*

*She struggled to excite the speech centers in her brain. She must cry out. She must warn.*

*She forced the words out, forced the cotton wads into her mouth, past her lips. They came out all wrong, but she knew what she wanted to say. Not what they heard.*

*Kill . . . Iscaaron.*

Joan's room was converted into a makeshift dormitory. Mattresses were slid from beds and twisted through doorways, spaced around her room, and made up by Mrs. Dailey. Patty and Tom would sleep there. Bernice Baines was dead on her feet, and they made a bed up for her. Stan Morgan's mattress was also brought in so that he could be at Joan's bedside in seconds should she show any further change. Kim moved her sleeping quarters, as well. This was all done with a minimum of noise, with an urgency resembling wartime or, as Mrs. Dailey commented, "Like when a tormado was a-coming." Francine Arnold would be awake throughout the night. Patty would keep her company until she became too sleepy;

then Tom would take over. Kim would relieve him if he wanted her to.

There had been no change in Joan's condition since the first rise in temperature and increase in pulse. Yet Patty was excited, hopeful. It had been Chill's suggestion that the beds be brought in, and she had instantly approved the idea.

The Bransons had retired to their room with iced teas and fans brought out of storage to stir the heat around. It was sweltering throughout the house.

Chill, Hal, and Laura snacked in the kitchen on a cold salad that Chill prepared, sprinkled with cashews and sesame sticks. They drank cool mellow mint herb tea and devoured orange sherbet that Laura found in the freezer. They didn't talk about Joan or the séance while downstairs, but it was on their minds. Chill knew that every moment now was crucial. Joan was coming out of hibernation. The crisis could come anytime within twenty-four hours—tonight or tomorrow or the next night. It could come at anytime, but it would come.

The question in his mind was how complete was Joan's possession at present? Was she being kept in a state of suspended animation only until a karmic prophecy could be accomplished? Or was she already invaded by a demon named Iscaaron? He had the strong feeling that she was still herself, that the possession had not yet occurred. He based this assumption on the fact that they had so far been able to counteract the encroachment of the algae. She was stirring from her deep sleep. The transfer, the metempsychosis, would take place when she was fully conscious. Tomorrow he knew he'd have to inspect the tomb. That was the key, he was sure.

That was where Grandier was buried.

It was late when the three of them entered Chill's room. The house was still, the heat less oppressive with the windows open and a fan running. Chill turned on only the lamp over the desk. He and Hal moved chairs over near the loveseat, where he wanted Laura to sit. They sat down, finally, in the darkest corner of his room, prepared to delve into the unknown.

"What are you after?" Hal asked.

"I think," Chill replied, "that we have to let Laura carry the ball on this. I'm mainly concerned about the karmic match-up between Grandier and Joan Brunswick. And is it inevitable? Can we break the chain? Is there someone else who lived in the seventeenth century who was close to the events at Loudun and who wants to see this match-up thwarted? I hope we can find out if Joan is now possessed . . . or about to be possessed."

"That's a lot," Laura said.

"If you focus in on the right person, it's not so much. I'm hoping Gen can find the spirit we're looking for."

Laura's blue eyes sparkled. She smiled grimly at Chill and took a deep breath. She had prepared herself for this ordeal. It was never easy to turn her body over to unseen forces over which she had no control. Yet she willingly did it for Chill and for Hal, too, who still grieved for his dead son.

As a medium, Laura was exceptional. She was clairvoyant, audiovoyant, and telepathic in the conscious state. Her father had told her that her gift was inherited from her Sioux ancestors. He said his people long ago talked with the spirits. They believed in them. Indeed, they believed that all things were alive in one form or another. But it was Gen, as she now called her mother, who acted as guide or control in all of her trances. Gen made contacts on the other side of the veil. Laura relied exclusively on her own powers. Unlike Chill and Hal, she did no outside reading on occult matters.

What she knew, she knew only through her contact with others. She believed she must keep her mind free of all influences, if possible. She observed and received. When in a trance, she allowed her body and mind to be taken over by her contacts in the spirit world. She had no recollection of what had transpired in this state after she awakened, other than a vague wisp of memory.

Laura had never worked with other investigators. She believed in Chill and what he did. She trusted him. More than that, she was entirely devoted to him—deeply.

Laura was aware of the dangers of going into a trance, of summoning up someone from the spirit world. She trusted Gen and she trusted Chill. But she knew that the possibility of possession was always present. It was something her father had warned her about many times. Chill was her life preserver. She relied on him to determine when she was in danger and to bring her out of her trance. In everything else, she was independent. But when she was not herself, she put her life in Chill's hands. It was a responsibility that he took most seriously.

"I'm ready," Laura said, taking a deep breath. She sat up straight in the loveseat, her shoulders back, her arms relaxed and hanging at her sides, wrists and hands on her legs. She wore shorts and a shell top, no jewelry beyond the amulet. Her black hair was tied back with an elastic band.

Chill lifted her hands in his. He looked deeply into her eyes.

Hal readied a notebook and poised his ballpoint pen over it. He had already written the date, time, and location at the top of the sheet. He had also written the names of those present. His pipe and pouch were stuffed inside his belt. He would not smoke during the séance.

Laura's eyes wavered. The lids closed. She fell back against the loveseat, her body limp. Her breathing deepened, becoming rhythmic. Chill held onto her hands, then released them as she gave up her energies to the trance state.

"Gen?" Chill asked tentatively. "Gen, are you there?"

The only sound was the hum of the fan in another part of the room.

Hal and Chill waited.

Laura's face began to soften, to change. It was as if unseen forces were working the clay of her flesh with invisible fingers. Her lips, full and rosy, thinned and widened. Her high cheekbones seemed to diminish and mold into the flatter contours of her face. The shadows of the room conspired to complete the illusion. Laura's face *had* changed. Her mouth began to tremble slightly. Her neck muscles became taut as her vocal chords shifted and strained to force the wind through them to make sounds.

"Hello, doctor." The voice was not Laura's. It was a soft, feminine voice, sounding tired, but pleasant.

"Gen?"

"Gen is here now," the voice said.

"You know what we want?"

"Someone at Loudun. A long time past, by your standards."

"Yes. Someone who knows about Joan of the Angels. About Grandier."

Hal let out a breath. He had written everything down, but his nerves were on edge, as they always were during one of Laura's trances. Sweat dripped down onto the tablet. His knees shook slightly. Chill looked at him a moment and smiled. Then he shifted his attention back to Laura. Her face contorted again, twisting out of shape as if her molecules were being shifted by a hidden force. The tautness went out of her neck. Her body seemed to shrivel, to grow smaller. It was a fascinating metamorphosis. Her eyebrows shrank, and furrows appeared over them. She began to pout, her chin receded. Her shoulders hunched forward. She looked, Chill thought, like a humble person, a beggar, perhaps, or a woman of the cloth.

"*Je suis ici,*" the voice said. It came through Laura's lips in a higher pitch than Gen's, a faint, hesitant voice.

"Can you speak to us in English?" Chill asked.

"*Mais, oui.* I am called Dampierre. Sister Urseline."

"Dampierre. The Dampierre nun at Loudun, sister-in-law of Laubardemont," said Hal. "You know about Urbain Grandier and Joan of the Angels?"

"I know them, of course."

"Where are they?"

"Father Grandier was burned. Sister Joan died holy. They are not here."

"Are they on this side?" Chill leaned forward, his attention riveted on Laura's changing features.

"*Oui, monsieur.* Sister Joan is sleeping. Father Grandier is in another form. He has been murdered again."

"Murdered? By whom?"

178

"By another man who was at Loudun. The Capuchin. Tranquille."

Hal's ballpoint raced rapidly over the lines on the tablet. His hand was shaking.

"The Capuchin Tranquille is here? Alive?"

"What you call alive. Yes. He is most dangerous." The speaker's English was heavily accented, the *r*'s soft, the *s*'s sounding like *z*'s.

"Why is he here?"

"He wants the land. He wants his inheritance."

"Was he mentioned in Grandier's will?"

*"No. He is connected with the will."*

Chill leaned closer to Laura. His eyes burned intensely. He wanted to be very careful of his questions. He knew that he could lose contact at any time.

"What is his name in this life?" he asked.

"You know it."

"Do I? Is he in this house?"

"No. He is not in the house. He is in another's house. He does not know who he is. Who he was."

"He is reincarnated, but doesn't know his connection with Grandier?"

"But you are very right, *monsieur*. He tortured Father Grandier. He was a cruel man. He burned him alive."

"His name. I need his name, Sister."

"Tranquille."

"Is that his name now?"

"The mother knows. The daughter knows. The daughter has another name."

Exasperated, Chill leaned back in his chair. Sometimes, he knew, the spirits played dumb or played tricks. Sometimes it was difficult for them to understand or to communicate. He felt that this was one of those occasions. Was she talking about Patty and

179

Joan? Did he know the person who had been Tranquille? The entity had said that he did. Yet he couldn't imagine who it might be.

"Don't you know the person's name in this life?"

"He will kill. He has killed."

"His name? Please! I need his name!"

"Ah, but you know his name. See the black man."

"What black man?"

"The *noir*. See the black man. *Bon soir, monsieur. Le Dieu est bon.*"

"Come back," Chill pleaded. "Have you been on this side?"

The Dampierre nun's voice was fading. "Once . . . I was murdered . . . as a child . . ."

Chill knew it was too late. The last words seemed to have come from very far away. Laura slumped on the seat.

Chill expected Laura's control, Gen, to take over her body once again. Hal shifted his position on his chair. His pipe was digging into his midsection, making him uncomfortable.

Something was happening to Laura that Chill didn't like. Her face was not softening as he had expected, but contorting violently. Her arms went rigid and then made grotesque motions in the air. Her body twisted and writhed on the love seat. Chill's eyes narrowed as he watched the hideous convulsions. It was as if some unseen presence was entering Laura's body, changing it to suit its own proportions.

"What's happening to Laura?" Hal spluttered.

Chill reached out for her, tried to grasp her arms. One of her hands struck him violently in the mouth, drawing blood.

"Laura!" he shouted. He rose from his chair and tried again to grasp her flailing arms. Her fingers

180

clawed at his face. He jerked her to her feet, grasping her forearms tightly. Hal rose from his chair, dropping his pad and pen to the floor. His face blanched as he watched the strange combat between his two closest friends.

Chill wrestled with Laura, whose body was now engaged in a frenzied dance. She tried to strike at him, tried to push him away, tried to free herself from his tightening grip. With an effort, Chill managed to hold on, but she had driven him halfway across the room before he could stop her rush. She was strong, very strong, and seemed to be gripped with a violent hysteria.

Then her eyes opened. They were glazed, red where the whites were, the blue of the irises faded to a dull luster. She hissed at him. A flood of obscenities issued from her mouth. She spoke in several tongues, some of them unrecognizable, some of them archaic. A torrent of filthy words rushed to his ears, making his stomach churn with disgust. Still, he fought her. He screamed at her, shook and twisted her as he forced her back toward the loveseat.

"Gen!" Chill finally shouted. "Gen! Help me! For God's sake, help Laura!"

As suddenly as it had happened, it stopped. The flood of obscenities shut off like a faucet. Laura's body went as limp as an emptied sack. Her face fell forward onto her chest. Chill had to stop his momentum to keep them both from falling in a heap on the loveseat.

He let her down gently. She was still unconscious.

He sat beside her and patted her cheeks, holding her head up. She took a deep breath and was able to support herself.

Finally, Laura opened her eyes. Their natural color

181

had returned. She sighed deeply and gave a half-hearted smile.

"Well?" she asked. "Did you find out anything? What's the matter with you two? You look like you've just seen a ghost!"

# CHAPTER TWENTY

Chill was up before dawn. He showered and dressed quickly, donning denim jeans, tough leather hiking boots with thick soles and a long-sleeved chambray shirt. He strapped on his Ruger stainless steel .22 pistol with the magnum chamber. He loaded the chambers with shotshells, for snakes. Just in case, he carried a snakebite kit—compact inside the rubber suction cup—and a small hunting knife with an elk-horn handle. The house had cooled considerably during the night, and he was relieved. He saw Nurse Baines on the stairs as he was leaving. She was bringing coffee up to Joan's room.

"How was the all-night vigil—how is she?" he asked her quietly.

"No change in her attitude," she said. "Her pulse is up slightly. She looks fine. It's cooler. Her temperature is still below normal."

"Thanks," he said. "Tell Dr. Morgan I'll talk to him later. There's something I want to discuss with him."

"Uh, where are you going, Chill?" she asked, shifting her weight on the stairs so that she could balance the tray of steaming coffee cups.

"Hunting," he smiled. He left her with a bewildered look on her face, bouncing down the stairs as lithely as a dancer. Bernice Baines muttered some-

183

thing and shook her head before she plodded up the stairs.

The morning was fresh, brilliant with a buttery sun. Steam rose from the garden, like the earth's breath. His shoes left fresh footprints in the wet grass and cut a swath through the weeds on the fringe of the lawn. He headed toward the bluffs, where the graveyard and Grandier tomb were located. He checked the strap on his pistol holster. It was fastened. He was glad he had brought the .22 along with the .357 magnum. One of his hobbies was building black-powder replicas, and he loved to hunt with the old-fashioned muzzleloaders. But he also loved fine guns and was a crack shot.

He was alert for snakes, but he wouldn't shoot one unless it was absolutely necessary. Once, he had narrowly missed being bitten by a cottonmouth, when he had stepped on it. The snake's head had shot up from the earth and twisted for a strike. Only a quick draw of his pistol had saved him that time. He had blown the snake's head off, but it was a close call. In snake country, a sidearm was a handy thing to have.

He crossed through the woods quickly, accompanied by the chatter of mockingbirds, the distant piping of bob white quail and the chatter and barks of startled fox squirrels. Blobs of what appeared to be saliva coated several blades of grass. The local people called it "snake-spit" and believed it was truly serpent's spittle.

He came into the open. A hummingbird, iridescent green in the flash of the morning sun, buzzed him, sounding like a hornet. He smiled. Everything was peaceful. The hummingbird fixed itself on a branch and cocked its head, eyeing the intruder. Chill knew

184

that the bird was a lookout. He walked on, leaving the bird to figure out whether he was hostile or not.

Chill didn't know exactly what he was looking for. He was just playing a strong hunch. He went to the tomb first. Even though it had been opened relatively recently, to admit the remains of Grandier, the tomb was heavily overgrown with vines. He pushed them aside to look at the steel door. They seemed to resist; they seemed to have a will of their own. There was a plate affixed to the door. It read simply: *Grandier*. The door and the heavy padlock both showed signs of rust.

Chill stepped back from the tomb. The vault was set into a hollow in the earth. He wondered if it had been drilled into the bluff. There was no way of telling from the outside. The sides of the mound were thickly overgrown, and he saw no reason to climb atop it. He went next to the graveyard, reading the names on the stones. Yesterday when he had been here, one of them had caught the corner of his eyes.

He found it again and read the inscription:

Henri Duchamps

1844–1890

He read other names and other inscriptions: Jacqueline Duchamps, Mère, and Lisa Duchamps, Fille; a Jacques Duchamps, Père—all born in the late 1800s, dying in the 1900s. Who were the Duchamps?

There were several Grandiers: Alexandre and Armand, a Maurice, a Lorraine, and a Marie. No Urbain. No Joan. There were other names there that were not of either family.

He was about to leave, when he saw some tombstones that showed recent care, in a far corner of the graveyard. He walked over to them. Wilted flowers, roses and gardenias, lay on the mound. There were three graves, each with a separate tombstone. The inscriptions startled him.

Papa Petitjean
Born: 1892     Died: 1970

Mama Petitjean
Born: 1898     Died: 1972

Rose Petitjean
Born: 1913     Died: 1966
Beloved wife of Moses

He looked more closely at the tombstones. They were made of wood, simulating marble. The carving was expert. Chill wondered if Moses had created them himself. They were the only grave markers that had crosses on them. And that's what had caught his eye.

He went back to the tomb and rattled the lock. It was very secure. Damn! He'd get Tom and Moses to open it for him. He wanted desperately to take a look inside.

Now something else bothered him. He had seen no fresh tracks in the graveyard itself, yet someone had been in the vicinity yesterday. Someone had sneaked up behind Ginger and pushed her into the swampy basin. The place to begin, he surmised, was at the basin. From there, he could backtrack in order to learn more about the person who had tried to either frighten or kill Ginger.

The tracks were there. They were made with the balls of the feet when the person had pushed Ginger. He backtracked, peering at the ground. At times,

Chill dropped to his knees to examine a clearly defined footprint. The tracks told him a few things: the person making them was probably small of stature, and the shoe size was a man's 7 or 8. Also, the bottoms of the shoes were smooth, not built for hiking in rough country. They probably belonged to someone from the city, although he didn't discount the fact that many boots also have smooth soles.

Once he had identified the prints as unique in the vicinity, the tracking became easier. The ground was moist enough to retain the impressions. Also, they demonstrated a definite purpose. They led somewhere. They had come from somewhere. He was surprised, however, to see that they led away from the mansion, deeper into the Grandier property. But they paralleled the bluffs. In some soft places, he saw the tracks of small animals, and once, the slither marks of a large snake.

The morning sun rose higher in the sky. Chill looked at his watch. He would have to get back soon. There were important things to go over with the various individuals involved in the bizarre events at the mansion.

He wondered how Laura was feeling this morning. She had been badly shaken when he told her what had happened to her during the séance. She had, of course, no recollection of her behavior nor of the various voices that spoke through her, nor of the strange manifestation that occurred after contact with the nun's spirit. He was certain that an evil spirit had tried to take possession of Laura's body. Whether this was a genuine attempt at permanent possession, or a warning, he wasn't sure. He knew now, however, that they were dealing with a powerful entity. He was counting on that brief preview as an indication that the spirit had not yet reached its full potential. Perhaps it had gained strength through Laura, or perhaps that had simply been an opportunity that presented itself and so was taken. He had seldom encountered such strength, such evil as he had last night. He credited Gen with intervening and driving the evil spirit away, and releasing Laura back to herself. It had been an incredibly close call. Laura probably didn't know herself how close, or how worried he actually had been. He had told her the facts, not what he surmised.

Moses figured somewhere in all this mystery. After the nun's warning, he was sure of it. But how? Why? The business of the grave markers bothered him. In the South, blacks had not been buried in white cemeteries. Of course, the burials were recent; that could explain it.

Were the Duchamps relatives of the Grandiers? They shared the same cemetery. Hadn't the attorney for the estate been a Duchamps? Pierre Duchamps. And he had mysteriously disappeared. Patty had not mentioned him as anything other than the attorney who handled the estate.

Loose threads dangled in the wind. They were elusive, but Chill was confident he could find the answers. What had the nun said? "See the black man," or words to that effect. Moses. Well, he had kept Moses on a back burner from the beginning. Moses was invisible except when there was trouble. Then, he seemed to be right in the middle of it.

The land sloped downward; the grass grew higher. Small clouds of mosquitoes rose up at every step. It was getting difficult to follow the tracks. Yet the grass itself showed signs of a person's passage, and that helped him on the path. The ground was swampy. He came to an opening in the sea of grass. The tracks criss-crossed all through it. Puzzled, Chill stopped and surveyed the terrain. The soil was very wet. Soggy, even—muddy. The mud was different colors. Some of it was light, like clay. Other spots were darker. He walked to one of these spots and picked up a chunk of the black clay. It oozed in his hand. He sniffed it. The smell was strong and unmistakable.

Oil!

Now that he had identified the sticky substance and isolated its smell, he was aware that the whole place reeked of petroleum. He was no geologist, but he recognized that this swampland was probably rich in oil deposits. It could prove to be a rich field, and it could mean a lot of money to someone. But not Tom and Patty Brunswick if they didn't know about it! Someone did know and was anxious to keep it a secret. Chill had to find that person.

He was glad now that he had left the house early. Cautiously, he encircled the swampy area to pick up the tracks where they entered from their original departure place. Chances were that no one was out here this early in the day, but he proceeded cautiously nevertheless. He kept low. The tracks led to an old road, now overgrown and, after a while, he became certain of where the old road would take him. He kept his eye on the sun, using the trees for cover as he continued following the tracks, which now boldly followed the road.

He was not surprised to be standing in back of Moses Petitjean's shack. The road had looped there, as he had expected it would. He stood behind a tree and surveyed the place for a long time. There was no sign of activity. Carefully, he inched forward, hunching low. A hound slunk around the corner of the house, its ribs showing through its hide. Chill froze. The dog saw him through rheumy, slobbering eyes, but it was too gaunt to waste an effort to wag its tail, growl, or bark. It found a wallow under the shack and fell into it. Its big wet eyes closed almost immediately. Chill let out his breath and stealthily moved closer to the house.

He covered the last few feet quickly, threading his way through empty coffee tins, a rusted plowshare, dog stool, and an assortment of broken-handled rakes and hoes. Flattening himself close to the rotting asphalt siding of the shack, he moved toward a window, which he took to be that of the bedroom. The inside shade wasn't pulled down all the way. It gave him an 8- or 10-inch viewing area. He peered inside the room, through the lowest corner of the window. He saw a bed with no one in it. There was no one, in fact, in the room. He moved on to another window, which probably belonged to another bedroom or a storage room. There was no way of telling. Junk was piled three-quarters of the way up. The glass was murky. The corners of the molding were thick with spider webs, both new and old.

He turned the corner of the house, nearly stepping on a cat that had come to investigate his movement. It eyed him suspiciously and moved out of his path as he continued on to another window. He glanced at the surrounding trees, listening to the steady hum of various birds and insects.

The side window afforded him a view inside. He saw the kitchen, dining area, and the living room. The table was jammed into a corner of the room, next to a low partition. Two chairs were pulled out from the table. There were signs of breakfast dishes. Chill's eyes narrowed. There were two cups, two plates, two bowls. Moses lived alone. Or did he?

Something else, too, caught his eye—on the table. A saucer in the center. Something dark jutting up over the edge. He squinted hard, straining to make out the object. It took several moments for the item to register. The stub of a cigar. And Moses didn't smoke. He remembered then that he had smelled cigar smoke at Moses' house the other day. So, that was it. Moses had company. And the tracks from the slough had led to the shack.

There was an eerie stillness inside the house. If no one was inside, where was Moses now? In his concentration on the questions bobbing up in his mind, Chill failed to hear a rustling movement behind him—the sound of cloth scraping against tree bark. He was still looking through the kitchen window when he heard the two clicks. He half turned before the voice halted him in mid-movement.

"What you snoopin' 'round here for? Keep them hands up above your waist. Come 'round real slow."

Chill raised his hands slightly and turned. He looked into the twin barrels of Moses' ancient shotgun with the outside hammers. Moses glared at him down the length of the pitted barrels.

"Hold on, Moses. I came here to talk to you."

"Sneaking round like that? Man, you lie in your teeth."

"All right. Put that shotgun down before it goes off."

The barrels dipped slightly.

"Please, Moses. It's hard to talk looking into the muzzles of that shotgun."

Moses held the shotgun waist high. He waited for Chill to speak.

191

"I was snooping. I admit it. I followed some tracks here. They weren't yours. Too small. You've got some-one staying with you. I'd like to hear about it. Who is he, Moses?"

"You da one better start answering questions, honky! What'd ya do with that girl?" The shotgun came up again to Moses' shoulder.

Chill knew he had to move fast. Moses was starting to shake, and the hammers were cocked. Chill dropped to his knees, his right hand clawing the strap over his pistol's hammer. At that moment, the first barrel of the shotgun went off. Chill rolled, drawing his pistol at the same instant.

"You rapin' honky bastard!" Moses yelled. He swung the shotgun wildly, as Chill scrambled to his feet, his pistol in hand.

"Don't do it!" Chill warned, but he knew it was too late. Moses' eyes were rolling wildly. He was bringing the barrels to bear for a second shot. Aiming at the black man's knees, Chill cocked the hammer back on the single action and squeezed the trigger. The hammer fell, touching off the rimfire. Moses fired, as well. A blast of air whipped at Chill's hair. Shot whistled over his head, turning his veins to icewater.

Moses screamed and dropped the shotgun, grab-bing for his injured knee. He howled and danced in a circle on his good leg. Chill rushed over to him.

"You aren't hurt, Moses," he said, his voice hard. "But you're going to hurt, if I don't get some an-swers!"

# CHAPTER TWENTY-ONE

"You done shot my leg off!" Moses wailed. Chill's fingers were steel talons in the black man's arm.

"Sit down," he commanded, pushing the black man to his haunches. He holstered the Ruger .22, leaving the strap unsnapped.

Moses squatted into an undignified position on the ground. He was sobbing, more in humiliation than pain, about the wrong that had been done him.

"Shut up!" Chill told him. "Roll up your pants leg. You're not hurt. You may have a few tiny little pellets in you, but you won't die from them."

Moses rolled up his trouser leg, moaning dramatically.

"See?" Chill pointed. "A few little pinpoints of blood. Dr. Morgan can give you an antitetanus shot, put some iodine on those spots, and you'll be good as new."

Moses saw the validity of Chill's diagnosis. The pain wasn't so bad now. Most of the shot had missed him. Only a few #12 pellets had broken the skin.

"I don't need no shot!" he asserted.

"All right. Listen to me. What's this about a girl? A rape? What are you getting at?"

"Man, we been looking all over for you. That white girl what done got herself in trouble yesterday done gone again. Her mother screaming that you done it. You the only one gone, and the girl gone too. Her daddy believes it, too. They out combing the brush for your hide."

Chill helped Moses to his feet. Moses stood there like a newborn giraffe while Chill picked up the shotgun and leaned it against the porch.

"You won't be needing that," Chill said.

"Say, what kind of gun you have there that shoots beestings into a man?"

"It's for snakes. You want to tell me about Pierre Duchamps, the lawyer, while we walk back to the main house?"

Moses looked at Chill with new respect. He favored his shot leg, but he kept up with Chill as the investigator stepped out toward the mansion.

"They gonna skin you alive, you know that? You know about Duchamps, do you? He want this place awful bad. He gonna get it too, I think. He made me hide him out. Promised me some money. Big money."

"Did you tell him about the oil, or did he find out for himself?"

"He knew about it. Before Misah Grandier passed on."

"How long have you known about it?"

"It's been seeping up there a year or so. I didn't know it was oil. I thought it was just a mess out there."

"Pollution."

"Yeah, that's it."

The two men went slowly down the road. Chill knew that Moses' leg would start to hurt after a while. It was likely that some of the tiny pellets had struck the shin bone. The lanky black man was excited now, half in shock. Chill was pretty sure that he

194

had gone along with Duchamps because Duchamps had threatened him, not because he wished for personal gain. Still, it was something he had to find out.

"Did Duchamps make you hide out, or did you seek to benefit if he took over the property?"

"He said nobody'd get hurt. He say they's a curse on this place. I know that for a fact, so I don't argue. Duchamps, he tell me this his place all along. He said the will left by Mistah Grandier leave it all to him."

"In case Patty Brunswick dies?"

"He never said that."

"But that's what he meant."

"He said Miss Joanie would die anyway."

"Did you believe him?"

Moses stopped in his tracks. He grabbed one of Chill's shoulders and leaned down, his face close to Chill's.

"You listen now, and you listen good. They's things been happening here a long time. I don't say nothing. I know Miss Joanie's real sick. I think she the cause of all the trouble heah. Listen, I like the girl. I like the missus, too. But ain't none of it going to be settled till those white folks out of here."

"Where's Duchamps now?" Chill asked, struck with a sudden thought.

"Why, he done gone out to that tomb of the Grandiers. He took my key. He said he going to burn it all up."

"Good Lord!" Chill exclaimed. "Did you ever think that he may be the one that's after Ginger? Come on, man! After you get fixed up by the doc, get out to that tomb! And tell the others!"

Chill left Moses far behind him as he raced for the tomb. If his hunch was right, there was no time to lose.

Chill was out of breath when he reached the sepulchre. He staggered into the clearing. His face was grimy with sweat, streaked where branches had slashed at his face. He wished he'd had time to run by the house and get Laura and Hal. It was too late for that now. The door to the tomb was open. He stopped and approached it warily, his right hand close to the butt of his revolver. The silence was eerie. It jangled in his brain like a billion far-off bells.

Even as he stood there motionless, the ground quivered beneath his feet. A surge of dizziness assailed him, fleeting, odd, as though an invisible force had passed through his body, taking something, leaving nothing. He closed his eyes briefly, seeking his inner strength. When he opened his eyes again, the tomb seemed to adjust itself with almost imperceptible movement, realigning its loosened mound with the settling earth. He knew it was only an optical illusion, but the illusion left him feeling even more uneasy than before. The vines that covered—no, smothered—the mound seemed to have thickened since earlier that morning. They groaned and writhed with malevolence. Of course, they weren't moving. That, too, was an illusion. He was being dramatic.

"Steady," he said out loud, as if to reassure himself that he still possessed his faculties, that he was still himself.

It helped. His mind began to clear. Yet there was something compelling about the open maw of the tomb. The black opening into the sepulchre was a magnet on his senses. He felt drawn to it, irresistibly. Yet at the same time, he was wary—not afraid, not quite. Not quite fearful. Wary—perhaps a trifle fearful. "Admit that much," he told himself.

In Chill's mind, there was only one way to conquer the feeling. Face it, head on.

He forced his feet to move. He forced himself to advance across the clearing toward the gaping emptiness of the tomb. Moses, he was sure, would alert everyone at the house. He hoped he still had some friends left. He didn't know what had happened after he had left that morning, but he could imagine. Nurse Baines had seen him on the stairs, seen him go out. Then Ginger had turned up missing. Thoughtless minds matched him with her disappearance. Fine. But what had really happened? Had she been compelled to return to this place, just as he was now compelled to walk right into the sepulchre?

His right hand hovered over the butt of the pistol. He wondered if he should replace the shotshells with the hollowpoints. His mind raced frantically. What was in the tomb? Coffins. The dead. Duchamps? Maybe. Duchamps couldn't hurt him, unless . . .

Duchamps was more of a mystery than Grandier at this point. Was he somehow tied in with the karmic recreation of Joan of the Angels and Grandier? Or was he unaware of his part in destiny? It was a maddening thoroughfare that his mind wandered, bewildering and incredible.

Chill shook his head as if to throw off these thoughts, which hindered him from meeting his fears face to face. The sun was now high in the morning sky, beating down on him, raising the scents of the earth in shimmering waves. He was surrounded by age-old vegetation surrendering their gases in a stifling, foggy mass that threatened to suffocate him. His dread was not of the tomb so much as it was the vast network of vines that closed around it, some of them hanging over the dark entrance like hangman's nooses, others poised like waiting pythons. He would feel more comfortable with a machete than with a .22 pistol and a hunting knife.

He walked toward the tomb's entrance purposefully now. He had sorted out his fears. The vines were merely vines, after all. The stench of composting vegetation just that. The tremors of the earth only a shifting of crust, a geologic occurrence. Nothing supernatural.

He stood in the entranceway, peering into the darkness. The smell was unpleasant, deathly, old, a contrast to the outside air, heavy as it was. He would have to have a flashlight.

"Duchamps?" he called, his voice echoing hollowly in the blackness of the sepulchre. He stood there, straining his ears.

He thought he heard something. He couldn't be sure. A moan, perhaps. A groaning of earth. His eyes could make out nothing. He stepped inside, the darkness complete, partly from the overhang of thick vines that partially covered the entrance, partly from the depth of the tomb itself.

"Ginger?"

Her jerked around, drawn to the sound of running from outside the tomb. Someone was coming! He stepped back outside, pushing aside vines that seemed to have thickened since he had passed through them seconds before. A large lizard fell on his shoulder, startling him. Reflexively, he smashed it off with the back of his hand, shuddering at the panic that had threatened him. He was as jittery as a kid in a haunted house. He ducked under the vines, into the open. Then he froze!

Less than 10 feet away stood Ozzie Branson, a gleaming stainless steel pistol in his hand, aimed straight at Chill's head. He recognized the Ruger .357 magnum. It was his own!

"Damn you, what have you done with my daughter, Chill?"

Ozzie's hand was shaking, his arm wavering from side to side. The man's shirttail was out, his trousers wrinkled, cluttered with stick-tights, his shoes grass-stained and muddy. His eyes were wild. Chill wondered if he had been drinking.

"Didn't Moses tell you, Ozzie? I haven't seen your daughter!"

"Liar! She left with you. Did you rape her before you killed her?" Branson was as close to hysteria as a man could get, Chill thought. He was irrational, and his finger seemed to be squeezing the trigger. Chill knew that trigger. It had a little over a 2-pound pull. It wouldn't take much to trip the double action.

"Get hold of yourself, man!" Chill warned. "Someone else has your daughter. I sent Moses back to the house to tell you."

"I haven't seen Moses. I just left the house. Ginger said she was going to find you this morning, to thank you for yesterday. She—she has a crush on you now. You took advantage of her! I'm going to blow you to hell, Chill—with your own gun! I found it in your room, you bastard!"

There was no more time to argue with Branson. Obviously, he was temporarily deranged. No amount of reasoning would appeal to him in his present state of mind. Branson's arm was steadying. His finger was tightening on the trigger.

Chill ducked low and hurled himself straight at Branson's legs. The .357 went off with a roar. Orange flames blossomed out of the muzzle. Chill heard the stinging whip of the bullet over his head as he fell short, sprawling into the mass of rotted leaves and loamy earth. But he kept going, scrambling on all fours until he reached the man's trousers. Another shot went off, high in the air, as he kept pushing forward, knocking Branson off-balance.

Branson fell backward, hitting the ground with a sickening thud. The pistol flew from his hand. Chill fought for leverage, struggling to get to his feet and subdue Branson before the man could do any damage. But Branson was fast. He kicked out with both feet as Chill tried to crawl over him. His shoes caught Chill in the gut, knocking the wind from him. He was hurled up and to the side. Branson was on him, fists flailing, striking home, thwacking into his face and neck.

Chill brought an open hand up, the fingers bent back. He shot the heel into Branson's jaw. The man's neck snapped backward, giving Chill a second's advantage. He squirmed from beneath the other's hulk, then rammed into the off-balance Branson, fists pounding into his kidneys. Branson turned around to face his adversary and struggled to his feet, his face grimacing in pain. Chill got up, too, keeping up his momentum. Pressing his advantage, he struck out at Branson's face. Branson was surprisingly strong, his strength fueled by his anger and madness. He countered some of Chill's blows, feinted low, and struck him a glancing blow on the forehead. Chill dodged the crossing left hand and arched one over Branson's arm, into his mouth. Blood flew as Branson's head twisted from the impact. Chill followed up his advantage, smashing hard fists into Branson's side and rib cage. Branson tried to twist back to face the onslaught and defend himself. Chill dove at him with a screaming right hand that split Branson's cheek from nose to ear. Blood flowed from the wound, and Branson went down in a heap.

Chill walked over and picked up the gun, sticking it inside his belt. He came back to the crumpled heap. Branson moaned and tried to wipe the blood off his teeth and lips. He was babbling to no one, and Chill realized that he had jarred something loose in the man. He felt sorry for him.

"No one's going to have her but me," Branson muttered. "Tom tried to get her. They all want her. But she wants me. I know she does. She knows how Clare is. She hates her mother. She loves me. I can't let anybody else get her. They would ruin her. She's mine, my own flesh and blood. I'll kill anyone who touches her!"

Branson looked up at Chill. His eyes were red-rimmed, his teeth bloody, his face covered with dirt and blood, the split on his cheekbone gushing blood with every breath, every movement. Chill was sickened by what he had heard. Branson had an incestuous desire for his own daughter. Yet it was obvious the man couldn't handle it. It was too much for him, the taboo too strong.

"You're a sick man, Branson. You'd better see a doctor. And while you're at it, a marriage counselor. Your daughter wants a loving father, not a father for a lover. She's attracted to older men because she's looking for a father. A real father."

Chill helped the man to his feet. Branson lapsed into deep sobbing. It hurt Chill to hear the racking sobs coming from the broken man. He grabbed Branson's arm, not roughly, but decisively.

"Get yourself together, Ozzie."

"My God, what have I done? Can you ever forgive me?"

The man looked at Chill with self-pity in his eyes, but with gratitude, too. His breath caught in his throat as he tried to stop sobbing. Chill patted him on the shoulder. They both heard the sound of crashing underbrush and running feet. A moment later, Tom, Hal, Laura, and Kim came dashing into the clearing, their faces stricken with alarm. The women were wearing tennis outfits. The men looked like lost refugees from a safari.

"We heard shots," Tom said, his voice breathless. "What the hell happened to you two?"

"Never mind that, Tom," Chill said. "Hal, you and Kim take Ozzie back to the house, and bring back some flashlights. Tom, we've got to go into that tomb. I think Ginger's in there."

"Ginger?"

"I think Duchamps, Pierre Duchamps, has her."

"Duchamps—the attorney? I thought he had disappeared!" Tom was as bewildered as any of them, but Chill didn't have time to explain.

"Did any of you see Moses back at the house? He was slightly wounded with bird shot in his leg."

"We just left there," Kim said, "when we heard the shots. Moses hasn't been seen since early this morning."

Chill's face clouded over.

"Hurry, then. Laura, you stay here. I'll find Ginger for you, Ozzie. Just get yourself together. Take care of your wife. Hal, keep your eyes peeled for Moses. I think he might be armed. No telling what he might do."

Hal and Kim put Ozzie between them, and the three made their way slowly back to the house.

"How's Joan?" Chill asked.

"Little change. The house isn't as hot as it was last

202

night. None of us slept much. Patty's not doing so well. I think she's closer to the edge than any of us realize, but Stan's keeping a close eye on her. Mrs. Dailey's about the only together person around."

Laura laughed. "She's baking a birthday cake for Joan. She's humming and singing, happy as a lark. I guess she's more optimistic than any of us."

"Good," said Chill.

"What's this about Moses?" Tom wanted to know.

Chill told them about his confrontation with Moses and, later on, with Ozzie.

"I think Duchamps has Ginger and that they're both in that tomb. I'm worried about the girl for more than one reason. These old tombs sometimes harbor deadly gases."

"Is it dangerous to go in there now?" asked Laura, looking at the opening.

"I don't know. I'm hoping it's had a chance to air out."

Tom looked at the entrance, too.

"Well, now we'll finally get the chance to see Patty's uncle's last resting place," he said. "The place gives me the willies."

As if in reply, a groaning earth tremor rippled under their feet. Laura looked at Chill, alarm in her startled eyes.

# CHAPTER TWENTY-TWO

Hal returned, bringing two flashlights. One was a five-cell aluminum cylindrical type with a large lens. The other was a plastic lantern that used a 6-volt square battery. Chill tested them both, flashing them inside the cave. They had powerful beams.

"Ozzie's babbling about what a great guy you are, Chill, and praying that his daughter is safe. What happened, anyway?"

"Long story," said Chill.

"You want me to go in there with you?" Hal asked.

Chill handed him the .357 magnum.

"No, just be prepared to use this if Moses shows up. He may have a double-barreled shotgun when he does. Wait here by the entrance. If I yell, you come a-running."

There were footprints in the outer part of the tomb. No caskets. He and Tom walked through the tunnel leading to the sepulchre which, Chill figured, must have been drilled out of the limestone itself. There were two sets of prints, both small. One was Ginger's, he was sure. The other was like those he had tracked all morning. Duchamps'.

There was another door at the end of the tunnel—it was made of steel or iron, and it was open. The two men went through. There was the strong smell of decay inside. Tom flashed his beam on the ceiling and sides of the sepulchre. This part of the tomb was concrete to keep the seepage to a minimum. Chill played the beam of his lantern over the smoothly finished walls.

"This is it," said Tom. "Where the Grandiers are buried."

Chill saw them. Coffins had slid from their stone and iron perches. He played his beam over the expensive caskets. The names were there. Bernard Grandier. Estelle Grandier. A smaller coffin was wedged behind the other two. Its top had been broken open by the fall, apparently. It was partially on, but crooked over the casket. It looked very old. The metal was covered with several layers of gray and green mold. It reeked of death and decay. A glistening salamander blinked sleepily in the glare of the light.

"I don't like it in here," Tom said.

"I would have expected more than three caskets," said Chill. He moved his beam to the other end of the room. It widened out into another, larger room. He couldn't see much from his position. He put the beam back down and walked over to the small casket. He had to push Bernard Grandier's casket out of the way to get at the small one. He grunted and shoved, moving the heavy casket to the side.

"What you got?" Tom asked, shining his light on the small casket.

"I don't know. Did the Grandiers have any children?"

"Not that I know of. No, I'm sure they didn't. Patty was their only living relative. That's why they left this white elephant to her."

Tom came closer, looking over Chill's shoulder at the small casket. The hinges had rusted away; he pushed the lid off, sliding it to the side. It clattered to the concrete floor, sounding strangely hollow. Both men shined their flashlights into the casket.

Tom uttered an oath under his breath.

Inside were the grisly remains of a young child. The short, dark hair was in pigtails. The ribbons had long since rotted away. There were gaps of skull between the strands of hair. The bones were small, indicating that it was probably the skeleton of a little girl. The skull grinned hideously back at them. The clothing had rotted away, too, probably from exposure to the air inside the sepulchre when the lid had been knocked off. There were bits and fragments in the casket, however. The child's hand was clutching what had once been a doll.

"Who is it? Or was it?" Tom asked.

Chill's mind went back to the day he had first talked to Moses. The black man had mentioned a daughter. Wilma. She had disappeared, he had said, when she was about seven. And what was it that the Dampierre nun had said? That she had come back once, but had died? No, that she had been murdered when she was a little girl. Had the nun been Wilma? Had Grandier murdered her? For revenge? It seemed likely, now. Grandier had murdered her. Because he had known who she really was. He had somehow recognized the little black Wilma as a threat. She had never had a chance in this reincarnation.

Chill grabbed up the coffin top. He played the beam over it. There was a small metal plaque. He rubbed it. The corrosion had turned what appeared to be brass or bronze a mottled green.

Then a name appeared.

*Wilma.* Chill sucked in a breath. So, Wilma was dead. But had Moses known that she was dead? He had said that she had disappeared. Didn't he know that she had died? Probably been murdered? Thinking back, he now believed that Moses hadn't known. If he had, he would have buried her in the family plot. But, then, why the name plate? None of it made sense, unless this was another example of Grandier's twisted method of revenge. Maybe Grandier wanted Moses to find this casket someday. Moses, or someone else.

"Well?" Tom asked, impatience tinging his voice.

"I think this is the corpse of a little girl. Wilma Petitjean. Her last name isn't here, but that's not surprising. I'm surprised her first name is."

"Whose little girl?"

"Moses', I think." Chill reached in and tenderly lifted up the skull. It had long since separated from the spinal column. His fingers went through the back of it. He turned it over in his hand, the beams of light criss-crossing it. There was a gaping hole in the back.

"Someone, Grandier probably, bashed her head in."

"Christ!"

"Let's check out that other room." Chill placed the skull carefully back in the casket and put the lid back on. There was no reason to tell Tom. The man he most wanted to see now, besides Duchamps, was Moses.

Chill entered the room first, followed by Tom. But Chill almost stumbled over a soft object. He heard an odd sound. He shot the beam of his flashlight down toward his feet.

"Ginger!"

"Ginger's here?" Tom bumped into Chill and couldn't see her at first. Chill dropped to his knees. Tom stepped around Chill, and then he saw her. Chill

207

felt her pulse and checked for broken bones. There were red marks and bruises on her neck.

"Is she still alive?" Tom's voice quavered.

"Yes. Tom, get her out of here right away." He had detected no broken bones, but her breathing was shallow, her pulse weak. "I'm going to look for Duchamps. Have Hal and Laura get her up to the house as quickly as they can. Then you wait for me to come out. Hurry!"

Tom held out his arms as Chill lifted the unconscious girl from underneath. Chill placed her in Tom's arms and patted him on the back. A moment later they were gone.

Chill splashed the large room with light. It, too, had been shored up with concrete. Yet a great deal of moisture had reached the inside. The walls were cracking. There were white roots jutting out of some of the crevices. A large spider crawled across the wall, blinded by the sudden light. Through a large opening at the far end, Chill saw a shape on the floor.

The man was small, dressed in an out-of-style pinstripe suit. Cigars jutted out of the handkerchief pocket in his suit coat. He had a thin moustache. Chill lifted up one hand and felt his pulse. The fingernails were neat and manicured. The hands were soft, almost feminine. The pulse was weak, so faint he could barely detect it. He turned the man over on his side and extracted his wallet from his back pocket. The cards told him who it was.

Pierre Duchamps!

Chill was sure that he was dying. His eyes were glazed, half open. The man's breath rattled in his throat. Faint wheezes could be heard in his lungs. Yet there were no visible marks on him, no abrasions. Chill rolled up his pants leg to see if there were snakebite impressions. Nothing. His symptoms indicated oxygen deprivation. He loosened the man's carefully knotted tie in an attempt to give him an easier time breathing.

He lifted the man up on his shoulders. He wasn't heavy. His body was entirely limp. He held the beam in front of himself and headed for the entrance. He wanted to get him to the house, too. Stan Morgan was going to be a busy man. He had no idea why Duchamps had come here, why he had brought Ginger here, why he'd tried to kill her. There had been a struggle in the room. But why hadn't Ginger been able to escape? Ginger wasn't as weak as Duchamps, but of course she was much younger. Both were unconscious. He had read something about the tombs . . . the Egyptian tombs. He tried to remember. It might help Dr. Morgan when he started examining Duchamps and Ginger.

He entered the sepulchre where the three caskets were stored. He paused for a moment, wondering at the significance of the casket with Wilma Petitjean's body in it. Did Moses know she was buried here? That she had been murdered? He had said she had disappeared, probably died. How long ago? Thirty years, perhaps. At least that. Maybe Moses just didn't remember.

Chill headed for the entrance. He never made it.

A deep rolling of the earth pitched him forward. It was all he could do to keep from throwing Duchamps' limp body into the wall. The tomb shuddered as the ominous rumble increased in intensity. There was a loud noise from above and in front of him, followed by a thunder of stones and a cloud of choking dust. Chill laid Duchamps on the floor and rushed to the entrance.

The door was blocked!

The air was already foul with dust; already there was a lack of oxygen in the sepulchre. Frantically, Chill dug at the earth. The vines were tangled, meshed inside the clogging soil. Every time he pulled at a handful of dirt, he encountered a vine. Yet he knew he had to get out, or he would suffocate. He climbed to the top. There was not so much dirt there. He began shoveling with his hands, tossing the dirt back into the tomb. If he could get only a little hole started, he could expand it, get air, eventually tunnel free.

"Laura!" he called. "Laura! Can you hear me?"

Had she left with Tom and Hal? Or was she still outside? He listened but heard nothing. The air seemed to have been sucked out of the sepulchre with the force of the cave-in. His lungs ached from the effort it took to breathe. Particles of dust floated in the little air that was left, gagging him, choking him. He pulled a handkerchief from his pocket, folded it once, and tied it over his mouth and nose. He continued to scoop the earth from the top of the pile.

"Chill! I'm out here!"

It was Laura's voice!

"At the top!" he yelled. "Dig from the top of the cave-in!"

Had she heard him? He heard her muffled voice, but could not be certain of her words. He knew he had to keep digging. He just hoped that she had understood his instructions. It seemed an interminable task. His hands became raw, his fingernails clogged with damp earth. After a while, they felt like useless clubs. Weariness settled into his shoulders, his arms. His chest ached with every breath. His mouth was dry, full of dust. His throat was raw with pain. He was unable to swallow.

Then he heard the sounds from the other side—from the top. He felt a renewal of strength surge through him. He found a perch atop the pile and began to dig like a badger, throwing the dirt between his legs, his hands digging faster and faster. Vines, rough-veined, thick and unyielding, fought him, tearing the flesh from the backs of his hands, ripping at his fingers as he clawed a widening hole. At times, he had to use his hunting knife, cutting through the thickest vines, chopping them up in sections.

Finally, he saw daylight. Air rushed in the opening, dashing against his face like surf spray. A moment later, he saw Laura's face peering at him from the other side.

"Oh, Chill! Are you all right? Hal and Tom are bringing shovels."

"I'm fine. I found Duchamps."

"Where is he?"

"He's out of it. I don't think he's going to make it."

"Here they come," she said. "Just take it easy. Let them do the digging. You look like a coal miner."

"I feel like one," he laughed.

It took the men twenty minutes to dig Chill out of the tomb. Tom had brought along a machete, and that had helped them hack through the tough vines. Chill lifted Duchamps up and pushed him through the opening. Hal and Tom pulled the unconscious man through, out into the open air.

"Did you feel the quake?" Chill wanted to know.

"Yes," said Hal. "We thought you might be in the tomb. It was the biggest one yet, Tom told me. Glad you're okay."

"Let's get Duchamps back to the house and have Morgan take a look at him."

Laura was solicitous of Chill on the way back, fussing over him and mocking his appearance. He didn't mind the attention. He had been very glad to see Laura's face at the other end of that hole.

"You can speak with Ginger shortly," Stan Morgan told Chillders. "She's conscious, but badly frightened. I'm having an ambulance pick up Duchamps as soon as it can get here. He's got to be isolated and treated. I doubt if he'll make it, though."

"Can I see him? I have to ask him a question or two." The two men were in the kitchen. Ginger had been taken to her room, and Duchamps was on a cot in the utility room. Nurse Baines was attending him. From her chair, she nodded at the two men.

"He's barely conscious now. You can try. It won't do him any more harm."

They walked into the utility room, which was large by any standards. It housed the linens and household supplies, as well as the laundry facilities. It was a clean, spacious room. Duchamps had been undressed and was wearing an old pair of Tom's pajamas. He had a needle in his arm. D5W solution flowed into his veins at a slow drip. His color was waxen. His chest rattled ominously when he breathed.

"Duchamps? Pierre Duchamps, can you hear me?" Chill leaned over the man. His eyelids fluttered and opened. He looked at Chill with dull eyes that seemed unable to focus. His breathing was rapid and he seemed to be in intense pain.

"We meet at last," the man said hoarsely. "Moses didn't get you."

"No. Do you know why Joan is sick? Why she's

212

been asleep? Can you help me? I know about the oil."

"Grandier evil. He wants her. I know who he really is. Was. Patty. Wanted to kill her. Then get property. Joan die anyway."

"You killed Grandier, didn't you?"

"You know. I'm dying now. The sepulchre."

Chill nodded, glancing up at Dr. Morgan, whose jaw was set grimly. Morgan had been the attending physician when Grandier had died.

"The will?" Does it say the property goes to you if Patty dies?"

"Yes. Only way I would execute it. Grandier stole this property from my family. Deed's wrong. His family got it. I found out. He paid me, but . . . I wanted property back. Because of the oil."

"Were you trying to kill Ginger—the girl you took into the tomb with you?"

"Hold her ransom. Kill Patty . . . and blame it on Grandier curse."

"You found out about Moses' daughter, Wilma? Did Grandier murder her?"

"Y—yes. Moses didn't know. Promised Moses a share of oil. He to kill Patty."

Chill stood up straight. Duchamps closed his eyes. Morgan felt his pulse.

"It's very weak. He's dying."

"I've got to find Moses and tell him that Duchamps has been found. He's wandering around with a shotgun— Where's Patty?"

"Upstairs with Joan. Come on."

They left the utility room. Nurse Baines watched them go. She hoped the ambulance would get there soon. Duchamps would either make it, or he wouldn't. In his present condition, it was impossible for him to

213

go anywhere. She wished she had a magazine to read.

"What happened to Duchamps exactly, doctor?" Chill asked as they crossed through the kitchen.

"Without knowing for sure, I'd say that he entered the part of the tomb where the air was old and foul. That's according to what you told me when you brought him back. The only thing that saved Ginger was that she was unconscious before he opened the other door."

"What are you getting at?"

"The old part of the tomb had been sealed off for a long time. The dead air was perfect for the development of *Cryptococcocus neoformans*, a fungoid saprophytic growth whose airborne spores are usually fatal, certainly crippling."

"In Duchamps' case they worked incredibly fast, apparently."

The two men stopped in the hall. Chill wanted to hear everything Morgan had to say.

"Go on," Chill said. "I've heard of this disease in connection with the opening of tombs in Egypt."

"That's where we learned of it. The spores are inhaled into the lungs, and the warm, moist condition of the pulmonary organs causes instant germination. The spores develop into dense, granulitic colonies that are highly toxic. The colonies grow like mold on the lung tissue, causing extensive lesions. Duchamps is hemorrhaging right now from these. His temperature is very high. His breathing is rapid and painful. The fungoid colonies generate wastes, which are quickly absorbed into the bloodstream and then, eventually, carried to the brain and to the central nervous system. You got your interview just in time, I would say."

"What happens next?"

"Oh, I'd say he'll have hallucinations as the wastes begin acting as a virulent neurotoxin. He'll develop a severe inflammation of the meninges. His brain will swell."

"He won't live?"

"I doubt it. But even if he does, he'll be a vegetable. Insane, probably. His lungs will be scarred. I won't know how he's forming antibodies until I get lab tests done on him. But from all indications, Duchamps has only a short time to live. The symptoms indicate that the toxins are forming very, very fast, for some reason. Faster than normal."

"Like the mold that kept coming into Joan's room," Chill said.

The two men looked at each other. Dr. Morgan bit his underlip. His eyes narrowed in thought.

# CHAPTER TWENTY-THREE

Patty was not in Joan's room.

"She left here a half-hour ago," Francine Arnold told Chill and Morgan.

"Where did she go?" asked Chill.

"Why, I don't really know. She must have gone to her room, I imagine. Oh, doctor. Your patient has had an abrupt rise in blood pressure and pulse rate. Would you like to see her chart?"

Nurse Arnold handed Morgan the chart. Chill looked closely at Joan, even though he knew he had to find out where Patty was before something happened. Moses was armed and didn't know Duchamps was dying and had told him everything. Somehow he had to prevent another tragedy. But Patty would have to wait a little while longer. Perhaps she was in her room, as the nurse had said.

"This is really extraordinary," the doctor said. "The change is quite dramatic, considering the previous readings. Incidentally, Chill, I did some checking with colleagues all morning, and it appears you were correct in your assumption about Joan's condition. But look here. Her pulse is 55. The blood pressure reading is 100 over 60. Remarkable."

"Has she spoken, Miss Arnold?" Chill wanted to know.

"No, but she has begun to move around. Scared me at first. All the goings on around here, and then Mrs. Brunswick left me alone. I didn't hear her speak or make any sound, but she definitely moved."

"What did your colleagues have to say about her condition, doctor?"

"There was a case of a British seaman admitted to a London Hospital in 1948, who had what appeared to be a neurological condition at first. He suffered periods of extended sleep and overeating over a five-year period. The diagnosis of Kleine-Levin syndrome was close, but it appears now that he was undergoing something more closely akin to hibernation."

"So you've changed your mind about Joan's condition?"

"Let's say I'm more amenable to the idea that she may be in a state of hibernation after observing her and speaking about her case—without mentioning her name, of course—with some trusted friends. One of them put me on to the work that a heart surgeon in Colorado—Henry Swan—is doing in the field of hibernation. Human hibernation."

"I've heard of him," Chill said. "Doesn't he favor a chemical theory for these types of symptoms?"

Morgan reached into his back pocket and extracted a small, narrow notebook. He flipped it open and riffled through the pages. Miss Arnold watched the two men, fascinated to be privy to a conversation about something she never would have believed before her experience with Joan Brunswick. Human hibernation.

"Dr. Swan believes that he's discovered a hibernation chemical. He calls it . . . let's see here . . . 'antabolone,' which is a combination term for anti-metabolic hormone.' He has isolated it in two crea-

217

tures—the African lungfish and the thirteen-lined ground squirrel."

"Didn't he journey up the Nile after that lungfish?"

"Yes, back in 1964, I believe. These odd eellike fish can survive for as long as two years, buried in mud as hard as concrete. Swan shipped the fish back to his laboratory in Colorado and discovered a way to strip the hibernating fish from its mud case. He would sever the head from the body before the condition of the brain had time to change. He prepared an extract of these fish brains and injected them intravenously into rats. This caused lethargy in the rats for up to a day's time.

"As for the squirrel, Swan can now surgically remove the brain and dip part of it into liquid nitrogen in about ninety seconds. From that mass, which includes the hypothalamus, he makes an extract that produces a state of pseudohibernation in rats for periods ranging from a little over an hour up to thirty hours."

"This research convinces you that Joan's condition is related to such a state?"

"It's possible. I don't know what triggered her hibernation, or pseudohibernation, but I'm convinced that the condition could occur in humans and most probably exists now in this sleeping girl."

"It doesn't help us much now, but I'm glad you did some checking. I read up some on this myself, but it's not nearly as convincing as what I've just heard. Thank you, doctor."

"Still, something's eating you, isn't it?"

"Yes."

Dr. Morgan turned to Nurse Arnold. "Will you leave us alone for a few minutes, please? I'll call you

218

when we're through. Would you mind waiting just outside the door?"

"Certainly not, doctor," Miss Arnold said. But she was pouting as she left the room.

After the door closed, Morgan turned back to Chill, keeping his voice low.

"It has something to do with what that man, Duchamps, said, doesn't it? About Grandier?"

"It does. You attended Grandier? What did you say was the cause of death?"

"Old age."

"Old age? Come on now, doctor! Is that what you wrote on the death certificate?"

"Well, no, obviously not. Coronary occlusion, I believe. Or cerebral stroke."

"Which was it?"

"I—I don't remember." Morgan was shaken, but Chill believed him. He probably didn't remember. In cases where elderly people died, the reasons given were usually good guesses. Very seldom was an autopsy performed. That's what bothered Chill.

"Duchamps said he killed Grandier."

"I know. It makes me sick. He could be hallucinating." Morgan was reaching for straws.

"I looked up the death certificate. It's on file."

"I know."

"The death certificate reads 'massive brain hemorrhage.' You signed it."

"So? He died of a brain hemorrhage. I saw no evidence of physical violence. Grandier called me, before he died, and said he was ill."

"What were his words, exactly, if you remember them?"

"Morgan thought for a moment.

"He said that he was very sick. He asked me to

come out. Come quick. I asked him what his symptoms were, and he told me. I'd have to look them up."

"Did he say anything about his eyes burning? His head aching? Difficulty breathing?"

"Yes, something like that. How do you know?"

"I don't. I'm just guessing. I think Duchamps planned to kill him, that he drugged him. Gave him a strong depressant. Perhaps Sparine or Thorazine or one of the other drugs that act on the muscles."

"How did you arrive at such a preposterous conclusion?"

"Duchamps' family, from what I gathered in the Shreveport Library, were pioneers in drug research and manufacture. Especially South American Indian preparations. Duchamps is listed in *Who's Who in Louisiana,* and he was attorney for his family's drug corporation."

"I guess I was aware of that."

"They marketed in foreign countries, mostly, but you must have come across the name in some of your medical literature."

"I recall it now. So what's the point? Duchamps drugged Grandier and then hit him with something? I saw no signs of contusions, no bruises on his head."

"I'm not surprised. Duchamps was smart. He could have caused a brain hemorrhage or a heart attack without hitting him over the head. He could have caused an embolism by injecting air in Grandier's veins. A doctor could have told him what to do—shown him how."

"Are you accusing me of complicity, Chill?"

"Oh, no, doctor, just stupidity."

Ginger smiled at Chill. He had managed to clean up before visiting her in her room. She was up, packing her bag. Ozzie had left them alone when Chill had arrived a few moments before. Clare was apparently talking to Kim and Laura downstairs in the den.

"Heavy stuff," Ginger said. "They think they can straighten Mom out so easy."

"You don't think so, obviously." He smiled when he said it.

"Mom? She's never going to change much. Besides, why should she? She's got Daddy wrapped around her little finger. She drinks all she wants, when she wants. If he says a word, she just shuts him out."

"Sounds like you know what's going on." He went to a chair and sat down. Ginger seemed to be packing just to keep busy while he was there. She moved from the dresser, to the open suitcase on the bed, and back, with slow, careful steps, as if she never wanted to finish packing.

"I guess you know. Daddy told me, well, some of what you guys talked about this morning. He says he's going to change."

"Did he tell you how he felt about you? Did he tell you he was confused about his relationship with you?"

"Not in so many words. Hey, you sound like a psychiatrist. They sent me to one once when I started raising Cain in school. He asked me about my daddy and my mom—all that stuff. I guess that's when I started reading up on stuff and found out I could turn Daddy on. At first, I was just testing—practicing, I guess." She sat down on the bed, holding a pair of socks, staring at them, stretching them between her hands, folding them, unfolding them. "I wanted to grow up, to find out things. I could see Daddy was uncomfortable, but I just wouldn't stop. I gave him peeks at me. Not on purpose at first, I don't think. Maybe. I saw his eyes pop, and I guess I learned something, yes. I tried it with other guys, older guys. I got a charge out of it. I never thought it would go so far. It was just a game. I didn't tell Daddy that, though. I think he's too shook up. I think he'd be grossed out if he knew all these things."

"Why are you telling me?"

"I don't know. You seem to know a lot. You're easy to talk to."

"You were looking for me this morning. I hope it wasn't to turn me on."

Ginger laughed harshly. She stretched the socks to their limit, then banged them silently together like a dead accordion. She looked up at him for a minute and blushed a pale rose.

"I gotta watch that. I almost got in trouble with Tom. I think I know what I've been doing. Would you believe Daddy told me? I want attention—from him. Not what you think. Not the sex thing. He was always so straight. He thinks like a law book, like Corbin's book of contracts. Everything logical. Well, life isn't that way. Then, my mom's drinking kept getting worse. I guess she saw something about me— about me and Daddy—that I didn't think she would. I couldn't stop what I was doing. It was attention. He noticed me. The wrong way, I see now. Not as a daughter, but as a woman. Not a very nice woman, either."

He saw that she was going to cry. He got up from the chair and walked over to the bed. He took the crumpled socks out of her hand and pulled her to her feet.

"Oh, Chill, I—I don't know what to say." The sobs

222

came then, rising up in her and bursting out in a rush of self-pity.

He patted the back of her head softly. "It's all right, Ginger. You're growing up. You don't have to explain yourself to anyone. I think you ought to talk to your mother sometime soon and get things straight with her. Don't explain yourself, just open yourself up. Let her know you. It might not be as difficult as you think. Your father understands some things now. You don't have to look for his attention, his affection anymore."

"I know. He's so good—so good to me. I feel like such a—such a dummy!"

He let her cry herself out, then released her.

"You'll be all right, Ginger. If you get stuck on anything, write or call me."

"I will," she said, drying her eyes. "Thank you. You've helped me more than you'll ever know."

He smiled warmly at her.

"I'll say good-bye before you go," he said.

She drew herself up and squared her shoulders. Her eyes were wet, but she was smiling.

"I guess I'm growing up."

"I guess you are, Ginger."

And then he was gone. He heard her humming to herself as he walked down the hall toward the stairway.

Clare was sober. Her face was puffy, and she had too much pancake on, but her eyes were clear, and she was steady on her feet. She and Ginger were saying good-bye to Laura, Kim, and Abigail. Hal and Chill stood together, watching Ozzie and Tom from a distance, talking just in earshot.

"We'll get together in New Orleans," Tom was telling Ozzie. "Bring your investors down, and we'll talk."

"I think I can wrap up the deal for you, Tom."

"I'm sure you can. When this is all over . . ."

"I hope Joan gets better soon. I'm sorry Patty's not here to say good-bye."

"She said she'd be right down, but she's exhausted. She was half asleep when I left her."

The two men shook hands. The women exchanged hugs and kisses. Ozzie got behind the wheel of his car. Ginger got in the back seat; Clare sat up front. The car drove away. Everyone waved. Tom walked over to Chill and Hal.

"He wants to put an investment package together for my next project," Tom said, obviously elated. "I think he has the connections. We're going to get together in about a month."

"Good for you, Tom. You know, you're a wealthy man, and you're always crying poor. I knew you wouldn't have any worries about your next project."

"That's why I'm rich, I guess," Tom laughed.

"Is Patty asleep?" Chill asked. "I wanted to talk to her."

"Was last time I looked. Why don't you go on up? Mrs. Dailey, how's lunch coming? It's almost two o'clock. Anybody else hungry?"

There was a chorus of assent. Mrs. Dailey assured them that lunch was ready and had been ready since noon. She had been interrupted when the ambulance came for Pierre Duchamps, but she had managed to make several ham sandwiches, a beet and garbanzo bean salad, and iced tea. She led the group, except for Chill, back into the house, explaining that people had to eat no matter how many emergencies occurred in a household.

Chill went straight up to Patty and Tom's room. The talk of food had made him hungry, so he munched on a sesame stick. He patted his flat stomach and wondered when he'd last had a complete meal. That was the beauty of being a vegetarian, however. He didn't get very hungry if he missed a meal or two. In fact, for some years, Chill had been in the habit of fasting at least one day a week. Every few months he'd fast for a week or so. That was something he kept to himself. Few people knew about it.

He tapped on the door.

"Who is it?" Patty called.

"Chill."

She let him in, holding a finger up to her lips in a signal for silence. She locked the door behind him.

"What's going on?" he said.

"I found it, Chill." She pointed to her dressing table.

"Found what?"

"My uncle's will. It was in Duchamps' coat pocket. I snuck it out. I wanted to read it first before anyone, even Tom, saw it."

She led him over to the dressing table, which apparently had been transplanted from Beverly Hills. It had a huge oval mirror, a glass top, and pink ruffles concealing the legs and empty space underneath. It was covered with few cosmetic items. Patty wasn't vain. Instead, she used it as a desk, for there were bills, contracts, a letter opener, and stacks of opened mail on it. In the midst of this was a folded packet of papers that Chill took to be Bernard Grandier's last will and testament.

She picked up the papers, which were stapled together, and handed them to him.

He read through them quickly.

"Aren't you glad you didn't know about this before?" he asked her, when he had finished.

"Yes. It gives me the horrors even now. Chill, I'm frightened. It almost sounds as though he wanted that disgusting lawyer Duchamps to murder me."

"I got that impression myself. Apparently Duchamps followed Grandier's instructions. That codicil wasn't to be delivered to you at all—the part that mentions that if you die, the entire estate is to revert to Duchamps."

"The part about Joan really bothers me. He discounted her entirely. It's like he expected her to disappear or to die. And Tom is to get nothing, despite any will of my own."

"Yes. Patty, I'm convinced after reading this that Grandier wanted to make sure Joan was buried in the same sepulchre where his body is now. I think he removed all of the other coffins from there years ago and kept that place for himself, for his reincarnation or whatever. He mentions in this will that she is to have been entombed there. But not you or Tom."

"Chill, have you seen Moses since this morning?"

"No, I haven't," he said. "I think Duchamps conned him into thinking he could share in the estate if . . . well, if things worked out the way the will is set up. I'm sure we can settle Moses down once he knows Duchamps is finished. Moses will get nothing if he tries anything."

Patty's face wrinkled up in worry. She put a hand on Chill's arm.

"It's worse than that," she said. "Look at this." She reached down into her bra and pulled forth a folded piece of paper. "I found this in Duchamps' coat pocket, too. It's another codicil."

Chill read it. It provided that if Duchamps, Patty,

226

and Tom all died prior to May 20 of this year, Moses Petitjean was to inherit the entire Grandier estate.

The codicil was witnessed and signed by Moses Petitjean!

# CHAPTER TWENTY-FOUR

The manifestations began that same afternoon.

The house began to move and creak. There was no earthquake as before, but only a subtle sickening movement of the foundation. Mrs. Dailey noticed it first, while she was making up the bedroom that had been occupied by the Bransons. The house gave a wrench, so she said later, and she was thrown to the floor, her pride damaged and her sense of balance more out of kilter than it had been during the previous quakes. When she had picked herself up and regained her equilibrium, a further shock to her senses sent her racing from the room in terror and howling at the top of her voice. All of the electrical outlets, switches, and plugs blew up in a sputter of showering sparks.

"Help us all!" she screamed. "God help us now!"

But there were problems throughout the house. A giant chandelier in the foyer fell, nearly hitting Kim. It shattered into a thousand pieces, while the old house shrieked as though it were in pain. Kim's usual aplomb was shattered along with the glass and crystal. All of the fuses blew. All electrical appliances stopped working, including the freezer and refrigerators. The natural-gas stove sprung a leak when the tubing was twisted and torn from its connection. Tom had to shut off the gas lines leading to the house. The acrid smell of the gas additive lingered in the kitchen for some time.

The din inside the house was unnerving. The house seemed to be protesting its existence. Every board gave off a sound of pain, each one at a different pitch. Gradually, the sounds became almost deafening. People were shouting at each other from various rooms in the house. Stan Morgan snapped at both nurses. Mrs. Dailey wept hysterically for anyone who would listen. Kim was still dazed and shaken by her close brush with either death or disfigurement. Patty was criticizing Dr. Morgan. Tom was cursing the house, the gas lines, and the chandelier. Hal smoked his pipe and tried to stay out of the way. Laura stayed with Chill, who paced the den, edgy but under control.

"Things are building to a crisis," Chill told her. "We've got to get everyone out of here."

But his decision was too late.

From Joan's room there came a chorus of shouts. Tom, Hal, Chill, and Laura nearly collided at the base of the stairs as they all rushed to get upstairs to Joan's room. Chill was the first to reach her door. The sounds of bedlam from inside twisted Chill's stomach into knots. He jerked the door open and rushed inside, followed by the others.

The room was a tangle of vines. They had streamed in through the window and spread out in all directions like ganglia. The vines were thick and alive, twisting, writhing, and slithering over the rug in angry whispers, entwining furniture, medical equipment— Joan's bed. Near the window in the path of the vines, Nurse Arnold lay, her face suffused with the cold blue of anoxia, her eyes bulging, staring, her body coiled round and round with dozens of them. Nearer the bed, Bernice Baines struggled with a dozen vines, her wind shut off by one that tightened around her neck like a python. Her blue eyes were glassy with fear.

On the other side of the bed, Dr. Morgan stood, abject with fear, his arms thrust out at his sides, protecting Patty, who shivered against the wall. The vines were snaking underneath the bed, moving toward them.

Joan was in the center of this nightmare, sitting up on her bed, shrieking in unknown tongues, spittle flowing down from the corners of her mouth. She seemed to be urging the vines on, pleading with them to kill anything in their path.

"Quick!" Chill yelled, hardly believing his eyes. "Patty! Dr. Morgan! Get over here!" He turned to Hal and the others. "Get out of here. Get machetes, knives—anything! Meet me downstairs. Don't ask questions!"

They did as Chill had ordered. Patty was hysterical and wouldn't leave, even though Morgan tore at her arms.

"Joan ! Stop it, stop it!" Patty screamed.

Chill vaulted over the tangle of writhing vines and came to Morgan's assistance. As he passed Nurse Baines, he reached down and jerked the strangling vine from her throat, pulling her to her feet and at the same time pushing her away from the other threatening vines. She managed to catch her breath and run from the room before the other vines could reach her. He got to Morgan's side, and together they wrestled Patty away from the wall. They carried her, kicking and screaming across the room, batting down vines that rose up like serpents to entangle them, to impede their progress.

230

"Get her out of the house," Chill told Morgan. "I'm going to try to save Joan if I can."

When the two were out of the room, Chill faced Joan, who had risen and was now standing on the bed, her face a mask of shining hatred. She cursed him in archaic French—spat at him like a hissing cat. She tore at her hair, crouched low, and eyed him while she spewed out filth in Latin, French, and English. Suddenly, the door opened, and Chill saw Morgan struggling to keep Patty out of her daughter's room.

"I want Joan. I want my daughter!" Patty screamed, running toward the bed.

Chill slapped her face and drove her back.

"That's not your daughter!" he said.

Patty collapsed in tears as the shock of what Chill had said hit her. She had seen her daughter. She had heard her. And Chill was right—that wasn't her daughter!

"Get her outside, Morgan."

"Good Lord!" the doctor said. "What is that in there?"

Chill turned back to Joan. She was transformed into a hideous demon, a grotesque caricature of the young girl she had been. Her hair was stringy and tangled, her face marked with deep lines that had not been there before. She was Joan becoming someone else, someone long dead, someone insane.

"I'm going to get you out of here," Chill said to Joan.

"Arrrrgghhh! No! Urbain! I want Urbain!"

Chill's blood ran cold. He shuddered as he watched her leap onto the floor in the midst of the vines. Nurse Arnold, her face frozen in horror, blue in death, turned over as if on a spit, as the vines continued to

231

tighten around her body and roll her before them. Chill took his eyes off the horror of the dead nurse and locked them onto Joan.

She advanced on him, crouching, leaping, her body strangely agile, quick. She circled him warily, her mouth full of the foam of anger. Her eyes glowed with lunacy, her mouth twisted in a snarl. Chill sensed that she wanted to get by him, that she wanted to get out of the house. He realized he had sensed it all along.

*It was time!*

He backed toward the door. Joan followed him in her animal crouch. He stopped. She stopped. He opened the door.

"Tom!" he yelled. His voice echoed inside the creaking house.

"Yes! What is it?" Tom answered from below.

"Get the cars started. I'm going to try and bring Joan down. We've got to get her out of here "

"Right! We've got the machetes!"

"Get the cars started! Get everybody outside! Hang onto the machetes!"

He heard running footsteps downstairs. Joan had advanced on him. She was less than 10 feet away. Her teeth were bared like fangs, the lips curled back hideously. Her fingers were distended like claws. She appeared like an animal about to pounce on him.

"Urbain!" she hissed. "I want Urbain!"

"No, Joan, no! He's dead. You'll die too if you go to him."

She snarled at him. Something he couldn't understand. He braced himself, sensing that she was about to rush at him. The vines rose in the air like hoses suddenly filling with water, rippling as they moved toward him, faster and faster. He was distracted.

232

Out of the corner of his eye, he saw Joan move.

She raced toward him with incredible speed. The vines seemed to flow with her, surging forward all at once. He knew it was futile to try to stop her. He threw out his arms, and she swept them aside. He fell backward as Joan leaped over him. He twisted and reached out for her, grasping an ankle. She turned and kicked him hard in the chest. The air went out of him. He felt something crawling up his leg, entwining around it. He lashed out with his foot and scrambled to his feet.

Joan was gone, racing down the stairs, her gown flowing behind her, ghostly white.

Chill kicked the vine from his leg, dashing after her as other vines lashed at his back.

"Stop her!" he yelled.

But there was only a hollow echo. The front door was open. As he bounded down the stairs, he saw Joan streak through the open door. A moment later he was on the porch. He saw them all out there in the driveway, stunned, their mouths open.

"Was that Joan?" asked Tom, his voice choked.

"Yes! We've got to get her. Which way did she go?"

Hal pointed to Chill's left. "Toward the sepulchre! She was headed for the tomb!"

"The cars won't start!" he heard Laura yelling. Hal rushed up to him, handing him a machete. He grabbed it and started running toward the side of the house. Others followed him. He turned the corner and saw the white wraith of Joan fleeing across the lawn, past the chinaberry tree, past the arbor, heading toward the forest.

To his left, Chill heard an agonized scream. He stopped in his tracks. The others caught up to him.

Abigail Dailey was trying to get out the side door

233

that led from the kitchen. She was a mass of twisting, strangling vines. Hal rushed up and began hacking away at them. Mrs. Dailey's face was contorted in horror. Her screams shattered their ears. Tom came up to help, slashing right and left with his own machete. Chill threw his knife down and grabbed the woman by the shoulders. He pulled her away from the hacked vines. Her face was drained of blood. She fainted a moment later.

"Oh, thank God you got her free!" Laura exclaimed. "What's happening?"

Dr. Morgan and Patty came up. Patty was shaking. Morgan was frowning in disbelief. He seemed to be in a state of shock.

"Take care of Mrs. Dailey, doctor," Chill ordered. "Patty, you help him. We're going after Joan."

"Let me go, too," Patty pleaded.

"No!" Chill was adamant. "Stay away from the house—and wait for us!"

"Look at those vines, will you?" Hal said.

Vines, thousands of them, had grown up the side of the house. This was the side where Joan's bedroom was. The vines were thrashing against the house, hooked up to it like a thousand umbilical cords, pulsating with evil. The view of the wall was almost obliterated by them. Some were climbing up over the roof, others around the sides, encircling the house as if to squeeze it to a shambles.

"None of us were supposed to get away from this place," Chill said. "We were supposed to be inside that house."

"How awful," said Kim, whom nobody had noticed before now. "And look out there!"

The yard where Joan had fled moments before was

234

crawling with vines. They seemed to have come out of the woods. They were everywhere, like snakes.

"Quick! Before they close off the path," Chill yelled, grabbing his machete. "Kim, help Morgan and Patty. Be sure to stay well away from the house. Get on the road if you have to. Just stay away from the house!"

"I'm coming too," Laura said. "I've got a machete."

Chill had no time to argue with her. Tom and Hal joined them, running toward the woods. Chill led the way, leaping and bounding over the vines, hacking at others that rose up to block his way. The vines seemed to be coming from the direction of the sepulchre, but they were not as strong or as thick as those that laced the house. Chill wondered if the vines were infected with the same type of abnormal cells that Rudy had discovered in the algae samples. Nothing could grow that fast. Nothing on earth.

Their progress was easier in the woods. Chill slowed down so that the others could keep up. He didn't want anyone falling down, dying in agony as the nurse had. Ahead of him, he thought he saw Joan's gown flashing in between the trees. She was not running. He saw her, then. She was walking, slowly and steadfastly, like a sleepwalker.

"There she is, just up ahead," he whispered to Tom, who had caught up with him. "Don't make any more noise than you have to," he told the others. "Maybe we can catch her before she gets to the tomb."

"I see her," said Hal, peering through the branches.

"Me too," said Tom.

"Let's stay together," Chill said. From nowhere, a vine slithered up above him, slashing at his face. He whipped it aside and ducked under it. He tripped over another. It was not going to be easy.

Chill stepped up his pace, keeping the fleeting figure of Joan in sight. They were gaining on her. She was almost at the clearing. There were more vines now. He had to sidestep and hop over them. The others did the same, following his path closely.

Joan was in the clearing. Chill saw her stop and turn around. She seemed to be waiting for them.

"Joan?" Tom pleaded as they drew close.

Chill held out his hand. "Easy, Tom. Don't get your hopes up."

They came to the edge of the clearing. Joan stood there, her face transformed. She was beautiful. In her white gown, she looked like a young, innocent bride. She seemed to be smiling.

In a moment, Chill saw why she was smiling.

From behind a tree stepped Moses Petitjean, holding his double-barreled shotgun.

"Get back, white folks, get on back!" he ordered.

"Moses, drop that gun!" Chill replied.

In reply, Moses slowly raised the shotgun. Chill and the others shrank back, searching for cover, but afraid to set the black man off prematurely. Moses stood tall and proud, his dark face set in determination. It seemed as though he moved in slow motion. Chill crouched, afraid to make a sudden move. The shotgun moved up to Moses' shoulder. He steadied it. Beyond, still smiling, stood Joan, her gown clinging to her body, motionless in the breezeless air as dusk crawled along the bluffs and the sky.

But Moses never got to fire a shot. The vines behind him began to swirl up around him like an octopus' tentacles, smothering him. His shotgun was snatched away. He was thrown to the ground, screaming. A thick vine encircled his neck, shutting off his scream.

Behind him, Joan's laughter crackled insanely across the clearing, into the woods.

"Jesus!" Tom breathed. "Look at him. He hasn't got a chance."

Joan turned and walked toward the tomb.

"There she goes!" Laura exclaimed. "Stop her, Chill!"

Hal and Tom followed Chill as he rushed forward. They stopped to hack at the vines that were crushing the life out of Moses Petitjean.

Joan stopped at the entrance to the sepulchre.

"Don't let her go in there!" Laura said to Chill.

The ground thrashed with living vines as Chill started across the clearing, alone. They flayed at his body as he stalked through them, flashing his machete. They tore at his clothes, smashed at his flesh, tripped him, rose up to impede his progress. Joan seemed to be waiting for him at the tomb's entrance. He saw her hesitate, then step inside. He covered the last few feet in a series of bounds, ignoring the vines that whipped around him.

He grabbed her hand and looked into her eyes. She seemed to be pleading with him to rescue her. Yet she struggled to go into the tomb. He put his arms around her, crushing her body to his. Her features contorted as she struggled with something inside her, with something beyond her that beckoned to her relentlessly.

The tomb rumbled a hollow moan.

"No!" Chill screamed at the tomb. "Not this time, Grandier! You've lost!"

Laura cried out a warning to Chill, but he didn't hear her.

Joan seemed transfixed. Something, some force, seemed to pass through her body. She looked deep into the tomb, her eyes shining with understanding. Her body trembled. Chill felt heat rush into the flesh of her arms where his own touched her. Joan looked away from the tomb and into his eyes. Her eyes were no longer pleading. The feverish look on her face was gone. Color returned to her cheeks.

He jerked the girl back from the mouth of the sepulchre. She faltered in his arms then reeled backward suddenly as though struck by a blow. Her gown slid from her left shoulder. A tiny slash appeared under her exposed breast, flaring a fresh crimson. She went slack in his arms, unconscious.

Chill swooped the girl up in his arms and raced away from the tomb with her.

The sepulchre groaned and erupted like an exploding volcano.

"Run!" Chill panted as he came upon the others. Moses was dead. They had been too late to save him. His dark body lay in a tangle of vines, the breath crushed out of it. His lips were peeled back from his mouth in a hideous grin.

The earth trembled under their feet as they ran out of the clearing. Behind them the tomb caved in with a roar. They stopped and looked. A cloud of dust rose in the darkening air. The vines whispered to a stop and lay on the ground like harmless green confetti. There was another rumble as the bluff fell on top of the tomb, pouring over it like a river of stones.

Chill looked down at Joan's bared breast. The small semicircular wound had stopped bleeding.

He pulled her strap back over her shoulder.

There was a sudden rush of absolute silence.

# EPILOGUE

Dr. Stanley Morgan smiled as he put down his stethoscope.

"Nothing wrong with you, Joan. Except for that scar, you're none the worse." The scar was thin, the length of a pin, just over her heart.

"I still don't know everything that happened," she said.

Everyone in the room laughed.

"Neither do we," said Chill. "I have to mark this down as a case of possession, but I don't know exactly how we exorcised the demon that apparently tried to snatch you away from us."

Tom and Patty were beaming with pleasure. They helped Joan down from the table in Dr. Morgan's examining room. Kim gave Joan a peck on the cheek.

Everyone in the room knew that Joan had changed. She was no longer the shy, introverted girl waiting for destiny to sweep her away to an obscure fate. Rather, she seemed self-assured, confident, outgoing. It was a remarkable transformation.

"I—I want to thank you all for your birthday presents," she said. Her long blonde hair shone from the brushing she had given it that morning. Her cheeks were tinted with a healthy rose. Her eyes sparkled. "I especially like this turquoise and silver bracelet, Laura. It's so beautiful."

"I'm glad you like it, Joan." Laura gave the girl's hand a squeeze. "They say you should always give gifts that you like yourself. I like silver and turquoise. Or jade."

Joan laughed. The joy came through. She looked around the room.

"Oh," she said, "I don't know how I can thank you all. Well, you know. I won't forget any of you and what you've done for me and for my parents. Someday, maybe I'll understand it. I don't know where I was, but I'm glad somebody brought me back. It was very dark where I was."

"You did it, Chill," Laura said. "You brought her back. It was a miracle."

"She wanted to come back. When she hesitated there at the tomb, I knew the possession wasn't that strong. You were the strong one, Joan."

"Both of you were strong," said Hal. "I never saw anything like it."

"Well, I don't think you have to worry anymore, Joan," Chill said. "You'll have some memories, but you'll be far away from the Grandier place. Tom couldn't have lasted long in the television business stuck way out there. He has to be where the action is."

"That's right. I know that now," Tom said, grinning.

"The oil can support some of his wilder adventures," Patty said. "But we're still going to get us a little place where I can have a garden. Probably in California."

"We're naming the oil well 'Angel Joan,'" said Tom. "For luck."

240

"Sounds like a winner," Chill said. "Well, good-bye, Dr. Morgan. Sorry I was rough on you."

Morgan stuck out his hand.

"I learned some things from you, Chill. I'm still trying to get it all sorted out."

Chill shook his hand warmly. "Me too," he said.

Kim, Laura, Hal, and Chill went outside, leaving the Brunswicks to talk to Dr. Morgan.

"Well, I guess we're all set," Hal said. "One thing's been bothering me, though. Was Duchamps a reincarnation of someone from Loudun? I seem to remember something about that when Laura was in the trance."

"I think we can assume that Duchamps was involved, although he probably didn't understand it. Remember what the voice of the nun speaking through Laura said? About one other who was the Capuchin Tranquille. She said he didn't know. But she knew. The only one who fits is Duchamps. Poor bastard."

"He'll need a few more lifetimes to get straight," said Hal. Then, looking at his watch. "I wish we could all go back to Atlanta together. I have to get back to classes, but I could talk about this case for a week or two."

Chill looked at his watch. "Hey, I'd better get you two to the airport."

They drove to the airport, still talking about Joan and how well she looked. The authorities had been very curious about the number of deaths at the Grandier place, but Morgan had come through with death certificates that satisfied the investigators. No one wanted notoriety. The Louisianans were superstitious enough without adding to it, said a sheriff who summed up the official attitude. Duchamps had died and no one had claimed the body. The house could be salvaged and sold. Tom already had a new television project to work on, involving nature studies, which he was excited about. And Joan remembered little of what had happened.

"You're riding back with me?" Hal asked Laura at the airport. "I thought, well . . ."

Laura looked at Chill, her eyebrows raised. She was wearing her silver and turquoise jewelry and a yellow dress that complemented her olive skin. She looked, Chill thought, ravishing.

"I'm driving Kim on down to New Orleans, Hal," Chill said drily.

"Oh." Hal seemed to shrink into his clothes. There was nothing more to say. He had already said too much. He clamped his teeth down on his pipe and searched his pockets for a match.

"Do you have to drive to New Orleans right now?" Laura asked Chill.

"Well, there are some loose ends. With Tom . . ." Chill said lamely. He didn't want to hurt Laura, or make her feel uncomfortable.

"I know," said Laura, a trace of sarcasm in her voice.

"Laura, please," said Chill. "Don't—"

"I understand. Unfinished business."

"Stop it," he said, looking deep into her eyes.

Kim looked at them and decided to save the situation.

"If you're worried about me, Laura, forget it," she said. "Things have never worked out between Chill and me. I'm going to New Orleans, and my boyfriend is meeting me at my apartment."

Laura's eyes sparkled. Her smile was as much for Kim as it was for Chill.

242

Before she and Hal got on the plane, Laura pulled Chill aside.

"Look," she said. "I hope you have a good time in New Orleans. Really. I—I, there's so much I want to say, but I think you know what I mean. Call me when you get back?"

"I will," he said. "You know I will."

She tenderly put her hand on his arm.

"Chill, I'm so glad you're alive. You don't know how close you came back there."

"I was okay. It was Joan who was in trouble."

"No. You were the one in danger. One step more and it would have had you."

He looked at her, his eyes narrowing.

"I don't understand."

"Didn't you see it, Chill? It was there, reaching out for you."

He felt the hackles rise on his neck, his arms.

"You saw something?"

"Yes, didn't you hear me yelling at you?"

"No. I didn't. I was concentrating on Joan, I guess."

"I yelled. I saw him. It. Coming out of the girl's body while you were standing at the tomb. It—it had a knife in its hand."

That must have been when the mark appeared on Joan's breast. He hadn't seen anything. Maybe he had felt it. He was glad he didn't have any of Laura's psychic gifts. He wasn't so sure he would have wanted to see whatever it was that had escaped from Joan's body. There were some things it was best not to know—or to see.

He squeezed Laura's hand.

He wanted, then, to take her in his arms, blot out everything else. What had he been trying to prove anyway with Kim? Was he rationalizing to himself

243

that a promise was a promise? He was attracted to Kim and she would have given him this chance to redeem himself. She had no boyfriend meeting her in New Orleans. Would Laura's ESP divine that in time? One thing, he was not going to pursue Kim. It was better, in this case, to break a promise. Laura was a partner, and much more. Kim was only a friend.

His eyes met Laura's. He saw the understanding in her eyes. No strings. It wasn't that way between them. She knew how he felt about her. Someday . . . someday they would go beyond this, would make commitments to each other. But now was not the time. He felt something being tugged inside him. Laura could do that. She could do a lot of things to him that no one else could.

What had she said? That it was a miracle? That he had worked a miracle. It had been luck—and, something else. Laura pulling for him, giving him some of her energy, some of her bravery, some of her heart. A miracle? Yeah, sure.

Only, Laura was the miracle.

He knew that, for certain.

She was the miracle.

**KILLSHOT...**

**MORE THAN A GAME.**

The ultimate novel of
life and death.

Coming in January, 1979
from
Pinnacle Books

# The Pinnacle of
# ∽ Historical Romance ∽

| | | |
|---|---|---|
| ☐ *Love's Daring Dream*<br>    by Patricia Matthews | 40-346-1 | $2.25 |
| ☐ *Passion's Proud Captive*<br>    by Melissa Hepburne | 40-329-1 | $2.25 |
| ☐ *Samantha*<br>    by Angelica Aimes | 40-351-8 | $2.2[ |
| ☐ *In Savage Splendor*<br>    by Paula Fairman | 40-181-7 | $2.2[ |
| ☐ *Legacy of Windhaven*<br>    by Marie de Jourlet | 40-242-3 | $2.2[ |
| ☐ *Love, Forever More*<br>    by Patricia Matthews | 40-115-9 | $2.2[ |
| ☐ *Return to Wuthering Heights*<br>    by Anna L'Estrange | 40-133-7 | $1.95 |
| ☐ *Madelaina*<br>    by Michaela Morgan | 40-151-5 | $2.50 |
| ☐ *Storm Over Windhaven*<br>    by Marie de Jourlet | 40-518-9 | $2.2[ |
| ☐ *Forbidden Destiny*<br>    by Paula Fairman | 40-105-6 | $1.95 |
| ☐ *Love's Wildest Promise*<br>    by Patricia Matthews | 40-047-5 | $1.95 |
| ☐ *Windhaven Plantation*<br>    by Marie de Jourlet | 40-540-5 | $2.2[ |
| ☐ *Love's Avenging Heart*<br>    by Patricia Matthews | 250987-9 | $1.95 |